HARMONY

ALSO BY RITA MURPHY

★   ★   ★

NIGHT FLYING

BLACK ANGELS

HARMONY

Rita Murphy

Delacorte Press

Published by
Delacorte Press
an imprint of
Random House Children's Books
a division of Random House, Inc.
1540 Broadway
New York, New York 10036

Visit us on the Web! www.randomhouse.com/teens
Educators and librarians: For a variety of teaching tools,
visit us at www.randomhouse.com/teachers.

Library of Congress Cataloging-in-Publication Data
Murphy, Rita.
Harmony / Rita Murphy.
p. cm.
Summary: Found as a baby by an old farm couple in the Tennessee
mountains, Harmony has always been different, but when she begins
developing special powers, she wants nothing more than to be ordinary.
ISBN 0-385-72938-3 (trade) — ISBN 0-385-90069-4 (GLB)
[1. Mountain life—Tennessee—Fiction. 2.Psychokinesis—Fiction. 3. Aunts
and uncles—Fiction. 4. Tennessee—Fiction.] I. Title.
PZ7.M9549 Har 2002
[Fic]—dc21
2002001663

The text of this book is set in 11.5-point Janson Text.

Book design by Angela Carlino

Printed in the United States of America

October 2002

10 9 8 7 6 5 4 3 2 1

BVG

FOR MY EDITOR,
DIANA CAPRIOTTI

ACKNOWLEDGMENTS

The author would like to thank the Vermont Community Foundation for its generous support in the writing of this book, and Joan Bennett for the use of her cottage in the woods.

PROLOGUE

LONG AGO, WHEN the world was new, there were no stars to light the night sky. In those days, the people of the mountains planted and tended their corn in the cool of the evening, for they believed the spirits would bless it if they did so. With no light from the sky, however, it was difficult for them to see, and often their rows of corn grew crooked and too close together.

The people went to the wisewoman of the village and asked her to make prayers to the Great Mother for more light so that they could work well into the night. For many years the wisewoman prayed, but the night sky remained as dark as a piece of coal, and the people feared that the Great Mother had forsaken them.

Then one spring evening, as the villagers were struggling to put in their crop, a light flashed across the sky and landed in the middle of the cornfield. The people gathered around to find a small child standing among their rough furrows. She was a tiny thing made entirely of light, and she danced about on the dirt as if she weighed nothing at all. The wisewoman told the villagers to treat this child with great respect, as she was a gift that the Great Mother had sent in answer to their prayers.

That spring, the people did as the wisewoman had asked. They showed great respect for the child and let her dance about wherever she pleased. But by midsummer, the people began to grow impatient with her flitting movements and exuberant energy. "Your light is too bright. It hurts our eyes. Why don't you go sit under the gathering baskets and rest yourself?" The child did as she was told. The wisewoman watched all this, but she said nothing.

By harvesttime, the child's light had faded from too many days of sitting beneath the gathering baskets, and her dance had slowed until it was only a whisper of movement, like the wind above the earth. The people complained once again to the wisewoman, saying, "This child is no longer of any use to us. She cannot even cast the smallest ray of light."

One evening before the first frost, the wisewoman found the child huddling for warmth under a large basket. She turned over the basket, picked the child up in her arms and carried her north toward the edge of the world. When they reached the mountains, the wise-woman set the child on her feet. She poured corn seeds into the palm of the child's hand and told her that one made from the stars can never be bound to Earth. It was time for her to return to the Great Mother.

The child smiled and took a step, and then another. With each step she walked faster and faster, and then she began to run. She ran and ran until she ran off the edge of the world into the night sky, scattering corn seeds in a long trail behind her. Each of those seeds turned into a star, until the night sky was full of light and the dancing child sat among them. Loyal and stead-fast, she sits there still. They call her Polaris. The North Star.

★

CHAPTER ONE

★

I AM WHAT folks in the mountains refer to as a foundling, what the Cherokee call *oo-da-ni-ya-da*, an orphan. Uncle Felix was the one who found me. He was setting up his Harmony Box on the rise that last warm night of August when it happened.

For forty years, my uncle Felix has been trying to capture the sound planets make when they move by one another in space. He follows the theories of Pythagoras, who lived more than two thousand years ago and called this sound the harmony of the spheres. This is the music Felix listens for on a little black metal box he invented himself.

On clear nights, Felix sets up his Harmony Box, puts on his headset and sits on the rise until dawn. He searches for lost stars and comets with no names, and occasionally, if he's lucky, he comes home with at least one good recording of the wind through the trees.

On that particular August evening, Felix had also brought along his telescope to watch the Perseid meteor showers, which occur every year about that time. Felix said the sky was clear and filled with shooting stars, and as he was gazing up at the northern sky, one bright star fell and crashed to earth straight through the roof of my aunt Nettie Mae's chicken coop. Nettie Mae has had Rhode Island Reds and Black Austrolorps in that coop, but she'd never had a star before.

Felix found that star quite remarkable, but not as remarkable as what was lying beside it, naked and crowing louder than a rooster. And that was my first introduction to Felix McGillicuddy fifteen years ago.

From that moment on, Uncle Felix and Aunt Nettie Mae have raised me as their own. Felix is convinced I am a star child and insisted at first on naming me Arcturus, as that was the constellation he most accurately figures I must have fallen from. But Nettie Mae disagreed. She said no child, star or otherwise, should have to lug a name as heavy as Arcturus through life, so they came to a compromise.

They settled on Harmony for Felix's great passion and McClean for Nettie Mae's people, who have lived in these mountains for four generations. A name from both heaven and earth, they agreed, would keep me well grounded in the world.

★   ★   ★

Since I turned fourteen last August, however, I have felt less than grounded in the world. There is a restlessness inside me—a feeling I'm getting too big for my life. Growing right out of my skin. In fact, if I could zip myself open and step out, I would. In a second, I would.

I have been noticing things about myself lately that are . . . well . . . surprising, to say the least. I'm able to lay all the silverware on the table, for instance, and then think about where I want the forks and spoons and knives to go, and they just move beside the plates or onto a napkin. All I have to do is think about what I want and it happens. It's amazing in one way and scary in another.

So far, our cat, Fellini, is the only one who knows my secret. One afternoon shortly after my birthday, Fellini witnessed me making a fire in the fireplace without any matches. I was cold and too lazy to get up and make a fire myself, so I just sat in front of the pile of dry wood and thought of combustion. Within a minute the wood was smoking; within two minutes there was a roaring fire in the grate. Fellini hid under the bed and didn't come out for two days. She still refuses to sit on my lap. Nettie Mae thinks Fellini must have gotten into a patch of catnip, because she's never seen her act so peculiar.

I can't bring myself to tell Nettie Mae or Felix the truth about my new *abilities*, because I don't know what the truth is yet. I know what they'd do if they did find out, though. Nettie Mae would whip up a tea of oat straw and hops to settle my nerves, and Felix would say that he's been right all along and I am merely displaying the qualities of a star child. "Harmony," he'd say. "You are a gift from the stars. Who would expect anything different from you?" Then he would proceed to turn me into his new scientific project, and I'd end up spending the next year of my life sitting in his studio with electrodes pressed to my temples.

I don't want to be someone's scientific project or the subject of gossip, as I have been for years. I've already spent most of my life trying to live down the events of my birth as it is. I don't want to start all over again trying to convince people I'm not strange.

The truth is I actually find the whole thing kind of fascinating, if not bewildering. It's like holding a little seedling in my hand and hoping one day it will come to something, like a flower or a tomato plant or a tree. I'm just not ready to put that seedling in the ground yet and risk someone stepping on it. I want to hold it to myself awhile longer until I know what it's all about.

Besides, Felix and Nettie Mae have more important things to do than worry about how many spoons I can move or fires I can make with my mind. There's too much work to do on our farm as it is. Cutting wood and feeding chickens. Keeping the roof from leaking. Nettie Mae is both doctor and midwife. Her days are spent preparing herbal remedies and tending to sick folk. Felix has his inventions. I have my studies. And then there are the trees. We all have to take care of the trees.

★ ★ ★

Nettie Mae, Felix and I live in the very northeastern corner of Tennessee in the Hamlin Mountains on the edge of the national forest.

If you were to get down on your stomach in our backyard and spread yourself wide as a starfish, you could have your head in Virginia, one foot in North Carolina and the other foot in Tennessee all at the same time.

Our house is a two-room cabin—a small and unusual structure that Felix has been building for the past twenty-two years. It is never entirely finished and always in the process of becoming something else. Felix sculpted one half of the house out of clay he dug up from the bottom of the Mulachooki River. He molded the doorways into high arches and made the walls in my bedroom all curvy like the waves on an ocean.

When he finally ran out of clay, he built the other half of the house out of hickory saplings mortared together with mud, straw and clover honey, which attracts every bee in Hanover County. Nettie Mae couldn't wait for Felix to pronounce the house complete, so she went ahead and painted all the walls white on the inside to give the place some sense of uniformity. And for more light—as the trees tend to take all the light for themselves if they can manage it.

All around our house is a stand of white pines. Nettie

Mae calls these trees the Old People, as they have been here longer than anyone else. Nettie Mae's mother, who was full-blooded Cherokee, left the Old People in the care of Nettie Mae when she died.

The Old People have been here for hundreds of years. When all the other trees around them were cut for timber or masts for ships, they were spared. They're ten feet wide and a hundred feet tall with branches that start thirty feet from the ground. We all love the trees, especially the biggest tree, Nula, whom we named in honor of Nettie Mae's Irish grandmother, Nula McClean.

Nettie Mae makes offerings to the Old People at the equinox and solstice. She leaves flowers, pieces of pumpkin bread and small pouches of Felix's Borkum Riff tobacco nestled in shells or wooden bowls on the ground. On windy nights, she sings her turtle song to them, invoking the soothing spirit of the animal who carries his home on his back. She sends her strange haunting melody high up into their branches. She'll even go out in her nightie in the cool evening air and pour water on their roots if they're getting parched. Nettie Mae says she can hear the Old People whispering among themselves, and she always knows if they are thirsty or weary from an eastern wind.

I believe as Nettie Mae does that it is our duty to protect the Old People as long as they are under our care, but lately that feels like a hard promise to keep. Though we live in the national forest and all the trees to the south of our house are protected by the laws of the United States, the Old People stand just to the east, a hundred yards from our front door. They lie outside the jurisdiction of the government and, therefore, are protected only by us.

To Nettie Mae the Old People are members of our family, but to the Great Northern Lumber Company of Tallahassee, Florida, they are merely good, soft pine wasting away in the woods when they could be chairs in the lobby of an elegant hotel down in Nashville.

★

CHAPTER
TWO

★

I HAD ALMOST convinced myself that Fellini and I would be the only ones to ever know the secret of my new abilities. That was before last Saturday, when I walked through the front door of my friend Shawnie Pawlett's house and set off all the smoke alarms on the first floor and blew up the microwave in her kitchen. Now Shawnie *and* Fellini and I know. And when it comes to secrets, Fellini is a lot more reliable.

Two weeks ago, I broke the Pawletts' toaster and a week before that their vacuum cleaner short-circuited when I walked by it. Shawnie had dismissed these as coincidences at the time. But no longer.

She scooted me outside onto the back porch, the

alarms buzzing in our ears, and held her wrist up to my forehead to check for fever.

"Feelin' all right, Harmony?" Shawnie wants to be a doctor one day, and is forever researching exotic diseases and human abnormalities of every kind.

"Yes," I said, taking her wrist off my forehead. "I feel just fine."

"Has this happened before?"

"A couple of times," I confessed. "It's no big deal."

"No big deal! Are you kidding? Why didn't you tell me sooner?" I shrugged. "Gosh, Harmony, how long have I known you, anyway?" She folded her arms across her chest and looked down her nose at me.

"Forever?" I said.

"That's right. Forever. If you've known a person forever and then suddenly they turn . . . *electric* . . . before your very eyes, I'd say that's a very big deal." She tossed her long red hair over her shoulder. Shawnie's tall and kind of gangly and whenever she gets serious about anything, her nose scrunches up and all her freckles align to the exact shape of the constellation Orion. I've never told her this, so as not to hurt her feelings, but every time it happens it makes me smile.

"I'm not . . . *electric*," I said. "I just have a little more energy than I know what to do with at the moment. It'll go away."

"Whoa!" Shawnie stared at me and her eyes grew wide.

"What?"

"That's exactly what *she* said."

"Who said?"

"This girl I read about in a book once. She could turn people into things, like insects and animals, just by pointing her finger at them. And she said it would go away. But you know what?"

I didn't want to know what. Shawnie had a way of making any situation seem far worse than it actually was. Once I made the mistake of telling her I had a sore throat and by the end of the school day, she'd almost convinced me I was dying of bubonic plague.

"It didn't go away."

"Really?" I wasn't surprised. Orion showed clearer than ever on Shawnie's nose.

"In fact, it got stronger and stronger and she couldn't stop it. And in the end . . ." Shawnie paused and her face flushed.

"And in the end . . . what?"

"Nothing." She put her hand over her mouth.

"Shawnie!"

"Sorry. Only I didn't remember until just now how it ended. It was a really good book, but the ending was a little . . . unusual."

"That's all right. I don't want to know anyway."

"A fly."

"What?"

"She accidently turned *herself* into a fly, and no one knew how to change her back. So she flew away . . . before her friends could eat her. It wasn't a very good ending. . . . But it's not like that would happen to you or anything. I mean, after all, what you can do is entirely different. Right? You can't turn people into things. Can you?" She pushed her glasses up on her nose, and her eyes sparkled like they did whenever she learned about some new virus.

I lifted my index finger and pointed it at her chest and she ducked.

"Cut it out, Harmony!"

"Don't worry," I said, lowering my finger. "I'm not going to turn you into anything. But if you tell anyone about this . . ." I raised my finger again.

"Okay! Okay, I promise. I swear on my aunt Tootie's grave I won't tell a soul. But you have to let me find out more. You can't just expect me to forget about this. I have to do some research. I mean, if it were me . . ." Shawnie stopped suddenly and her face fell. She sat down on the porch steps and let out a long sigh. I sat down next to her.

"What's the matter?"

"It's just that . . . all the really great stuff always happens to *you*."

"Oh, right, Shawnie, really great. I don't even know when it's going to happen. It's like having a tropical fever that comes on without warning. I could make a fool out of myself at any moment. It's not always great, Shawnie. Believe me."

"Just wait, you'll see. It'll all work out perfectly. You're charmed, Harmony. Just admit it. You lead a charmed life."

"That's not true."

"It is. Look at your nose."

"What about my nose?"

"It's perfect. A perfect little nose with no freckles. And thick blond hair that never gets stringy. Your uncle Felix thinks you're an angel or something that fell out of the sky, right? And now this. It's the coolest thing that could happen to a person."

Maybe if my life had started off in a more normal fashion, I would have agreed with Shawnie, but simply by the events of my birth, I've been set apart. Folks on the mountain don't condemn me for arriving the way I did, but they do tend to take a step or two back when they talk to me, and I've even seen women bless themselves after they leave our house, just to be safe. If they knew I could affect things with my mind, they'd start talking, and that talk would travel faster than the wind. They might start collecting their own herbs and delivering their own babies, or make the long drive to Doc Edwards's office over in Hildeen. That would make life difficult for Nettie Mae—for all of us. I hadn't any say about the story of my birth spreading like wildfire, but I do have a say about this.

"Shawnie, look at me." She looked up, her face as long as a hound dog's. "You have a lovely nose."

"I do not."

"You do. And your life is just as charmed as mine. I'm glad you think it's great I broke your microwave, but not everybody might think so. I don't want people knowing about it yet. Not until I have some time to

15

understand what it's all about myself. Okay?" I held out my hand. Shawnie stared at it.

"Is there more you can do, besides make alarms go off?"

"There is. I don't know how much more, but I'm sure I'll find out."

Shawnie's eyes got big and round. She took my hand and shook it three times. She spit behind her and I did the same, and we sealed the bargain like we did when we were five years old and promised to always stand by each other, no matter what. I could trust Shawnie to stick up for me, but I knew I couldn't expect her to keep a secret forever. I just hoped she wouldn't say anything for a little while, and I wouldn't turn her into a fly—at least not yet.

★

CHAPTER

THREE

★

A LETTER ARRIVED in this morning's mail. It was addressed to Nettie Mae McClean from Burston Jones, a lawyer in Carson City. Nettie Mae read us the letter while she fried up onions and a batch of parsnips for our supper. Nettie Mae knows every wild herb and root that grows in the mountains of northern Tennessee, and frequently cooks up any number of them for Felix and me to sample. Dandelion to support the liver, and wild leeks to purify the blood. Parsnip roots are her favorite. She can make anything out of parsnips. She even made parsnip pancakes one morning for breakfast, but they didn't come out too well. We ended up feeding them to our dog, Wilson.

"Listen here," Nettie Mae said, wiping onion tears from her eyes. She threw a pinch of coltsfoot into the parsnips for seasoning, slipped on her bifocals and leaned her tall frame into the doorway.

"Dear Ms. McClean:

I am writing to inform you that the Great Northern Lumber Company of Tallahassee, Florida, has recently purchased lot number 3098 adjacent to your property and will be exercising its rights to harvest timber on that land. Any questions or objections regarding this notice must be mailed to our office before the first day of the month. Harvesting is scheduled to begin no later than May 30.

Sincerely,

Burston C. Jones
Attorney at Law
Gadwick, Gadwick & Jones"

"Give that letter here, Nettie Mae," Felix said, pulling himself up taller in his chair by the fire and taking the letter from Nettie Mae's hand. Felix examined it like he examines everything. Slowly. He sniffed it and rubbed the fancy cream-colored parchment between his fingers, then laid the letter in his lap and stared at it for a long time.

"What do you make of it, Felix?" I asked, my eyes already burning from onions.

"Can't rightly say, Harmony. Looks official. Smells

all perfumey, like one of those fancy offices down in Carson City." Felix leaned back into the rocker and took a long drag on his pipe. Felix has a deep peace about him. Nettie Mae says the whole world could be going crazy and Felix McGillicuddy would be sitting in his chair, smoking on his pipe, contemplating the astral planes. All I have to do is stand beside Felix and I can feel that calm. It lifts off him in waves into the air, but it doesn't seem to reach Nettie Mae very often.

Nettie Mae worries. She worries about everything and everybody, and she works too hard. Some days, Felix and I won't catch sight of her until the early hours of the morning, riding home on our mule, Anthony, in the fog. Felix says Nettie Mae isn't strong enough anymore to be staying up all night, nursing sick folks like she does. He says it's not worth it, for what she gets in return. Old onions and sore feet. Folks up here don't have a lot, so Nettie Mae gets paid mostly with chickens and vegetables and an occasional deer during hunting season. Felix makes some money selling honey and cutting firewood, but we're not rich. Though we don't have a lot, Felix assures us that we're luckier than most because we have each other. "We'll do just fine," he says, "without Nettie Mae working herself to death." But Nettie Mae won't hear a word of it. She says that she's been given a gift to work the herbs and if she doesn't use it, she might just as well take to her bed right now and pass on to the other side. Felix and I know there's no point in arguing. Once Nettie Mae McClean makes up her mind, she rarely changes it.

Nettie Mae wiped her hands on her apron. "I'll tell you what this means," she said, her mouth puckered with worry. "It means they're going to come down here with their big machines and rip this land to shreds. They'll cut down the Old People as if they were nothing at all and haul them away."

Nettie Mae is a large-boned woman with a mess of curly gray locks on top of her head and a face as sweet as honey. She's like a tree herself. Tall and broad with a large canopy of waving leaves on top. But when Nettie Mae gets angry, her face twists all up, then turns to stone. Right then it looked harder than I'd ever seen it.

"Now, honey," Felix soothed. "Don't get yourself all worked up. Sit down and take the load off your feet." Nettie Mae folded her arms across her chest and stood her ground. She had no intention of sitting down anywhere.

"Nettie, don't go frettin' over a little letter, now. We won't let anybody take the Old People, will we, Harmony?" I shook my head. "Why, it could all be a mistake," Felix said.

Nettie Mae shook her head. "Mama left the Old People for me to watch over, but you know as well as I do, Felix, that we don't own any piece of paper to claim them. Just Mama's words. That's all I have. Just her words."

It's true that we don't own the land the Old People stand on. Nettie Mae says the spirits of the mountains own it and all the land around us, and are mighty nice to let us settle in here for a while. She says it is a false-hood to think that any one person could own a piece of the earth. "We're here for such a short time, Harmony," Nettie Mae told me once. "Too short a time to try and claim anything for ourselves."

"Why don't we just put this letter away for the evening, Nettie," Felix said as he placed it up on the mantel over the fireplace. He walked into the kitchen and grabbed Nettie Mae around the waist from behind, kissing her on the neck. "You know how I hate to get serious about anything on an empty stomach."

She swatted at his hand, but didn't push him away. A smile cracked the hardness of her face and she reached back and patted Felix's cheek.

"How about a little music?" Felix offered.

"A little music would be fine," she said.

Felix retrieved his fiddle from the top shelf of the pantry and opened the leather-bound case with his ini-tials, F.I.M., embossed on the side. Felix Ignatius McGillicuddy. The Ignatius was for his great-grandfather, who'd made the fiddle himself—carved it out of curly maple. Felix rubbed rosin on the bow and fit the end snugly under his arm.

There is nothing I love more than to sit by the fire and listen to Felix pull his bow across the strings. He plays exactly how you'd think he would: light and sweet and tender. His song lyrics, which he writes himself, are often ridiculous, and almost never rhyme. He wrote one song about an old man with three feet walking up a mountain blindfolded, and another about a girl with golden hair who kept a mouse up her sleeve—which is based on me. Though I never kept the mouse up my sleeve. I kept it in my pocket.

Even though Felix's songs make no sense, they are always played in perfect pitch. Felix loves the beauty and order of the natural world, and the music vibrating from his strings is just like the wind whistling or a lark singing—in harmony with everything around it. When Felix starts playing, any troubles I have are forgotten.

Felix played several songs before dinner, while Nettie Mae and I hummed along in the background. Before bed he told us the story of how his father saved him once when he almost fell off a lobster boat as a young boy. The evening was saved from worry by Felix's fiddle and his story, making any letter from a lawyer seem very small.

Felix believes that there is a way to turn any situation around in your favor. He's the kind of person who can go looking for four-leaf clovers in a field and find a whole fistful. It is his strong belief that we are relying upon to help us save the trees.

For now, Felix says we have to make it look like we don't care about the Old People—that it wouldn't bother us one lick if the bulldozers of the Great Northern Lumber Company came in and leveled every tree around these parts. "If they think we don't care," I heard Felix telling Nettie Mae that evening after I'd gone off to bed, "then they'll never suspect us."

★

CHAPTER FOUR

★

HE HAD DARK curly hair and a cleft in his chin. His eyes were brown, a deep, rich brown like a bag full of chestnuts. He sat next to Shawnie on the front steps of the schoolhouse.

"Harmony," Shawnie said, motioning me to her side. "I'd like to introduce you to my cousin Caleb. He's up from Delaware County helping my daddy with the haying this week."

"Hi," Caleb said, holding out his hand.

"Hi," I said, looking at my feet.

Nettie Mae says I'm downright pretty and have no reason to be shy of boys, but I am. Boys keep away from me and I keep away from them. That's the way it's always been. It's as if I have an invisible shield around me, fastened at birth, and except for Nettie Mae, Felix and Shawnie, no one else ever gets too close. If that's what Shawnie means by a charmed life, I guess that's what I have.

When I finally gathered the courage to look up again, Caleb was staring at me. He was tall and good-looking. He wore a clean pair of jeans, work boots and a white cotton shirt rolled up to the elbows that perfectly matched his teeth. I'd heard Shawnie talk about her cousin Caleb before, but she always goes down to visit him. She never mentioned that he was coming here and she never mentioned what he looked like.

"Harmony McClean is my bosom buddy. She's the girl I told you about, remember?"

"Oh, right, you're the one who can set microwaves on fire," he said, flashing his bright smile.

I felt heat rise to my cheeks and a burning sensation start in the pit of my stomach. I should have known Shawnie couldn't keep something as big as that to herself for longer than a week. I gave her a hard look and folded my arms across my chest.

"Now don't get your tail feathers up, Harmony," Shawnie said, blushing. "Caleb is family. And besides, he promised not to tell anyone," she said, giving him a nudge in the ribs.

"Just like *you* promised not to tell anyone?" I said, glaring at her. "How do I know loose tongues don't run in your family?"

Caleb's smile faded a little, and a serious expression flashed across his face. He has what Felix refers to as a mountain face—it can change like the weather in the mountains. One minute dark and stormy, and the next full of sunshine without a cloud in sight. Coming from the ocean, Felix finds these kinds of faces unsettling, but I prefer them. I like to see what someone is feeling right in plain view of the world.

"Don't worry, Harmony. Your secret is safe with me. I'm not loose-tongued like my cousin here. I'm a steel trap when it comes to other folks' secrets."

"I am *not* loose-tongued, Caleb. Take that back," Shawnie said in a pouty voice.

"Oh, no? What about Uncle Buddy's sheep?"

"Okay, okay," Shawnie said, a smile spreading across her face.

"What about his sheep?" I asked.

"Never you mind, Harmony, and don't you dare tell her, Caleb."

"Or else," they both said together, and then laughed.

I could tell that they'd probably spent their whole lives so far teasing each other. That's the one thing I miss—not having a brother or sister. No one to squabble with. No one to tease. No one who knows what I'm going to say before I say it myself.

"Do you forgive me?" Shawnie asked. Her freckles were all mixed up; I could barely make out Orion's belt. I hated to see her that way. She'd never rest until I forgave her. It was always like that. Neither of us was good at holding a grudge for long.

"Nobody else, Shawnie. Can you promise me that? No one." I raised my finger and pointed it at her chest.

She crossed her heart and put her hand over her mouth. "Not another soul, Harmony. I swear." Caleb smiled and winked at me as if to say, "Good luck."

★ ★ ★

To make up for telling Caleb, Shawnie invited me to her house every day after school that week so I could "run into" him. I knew what she was trying to do, but I didn't really mind. I sort of liked it.

I found myself distracted and kind of light-headed whenever I was around him. I forgot to feed the chickens in the morning, and left my books on the kitchen table two days in a row. When Friday finally rolled around, Nettie Mae threatened to keep me home from school until she figured out what strange disease was plaguing me. But there was nothing wrong with me. At least nothing Nettie Mae's herbs could cure. I'd finally met a boy who wasn't afraid of me.

Caleb and I talked about everything—school and the mountains and stars. He was interested in stars. I even told him about the trees, which surprised me. He promised not to tell anyone about our plans and I believed him. I knew he was the kind of person who kept his word.

For the first time in my life, I felt like I was beginning to fit in—I was no longer an outsider. When I wasn't with Shawnie, I was with Caleb. We did everything together that week, as if we'd been a threesome all our lives. As if it were the most natural thing in the world. But, along with my chores and my books, I'd forgotten about me. I'd forgotten how strange it was to not know what I was capable of, and to be able to make things happen even when I didn't want them to.

It was Friday, the last day Caleb was staying in the Hollow. He came to school that day to listen to old Ace Carver talk to our class about how to grow blue spruce in mountain soil.

Everything was going along fine until the end of the day when Mrs. Harner, our teacher, asked us all to stand in a circle, hold hands and sing "Happy Birthday" to Charlene Spooner. I stood between Mr. Carver and Caleb. I was nervous about holding Caleb's hand, so I reached out and took Mr. Carver's first, but as soon as I touched it I knew something was wrong. A shock spread up my left arm like a hot, searing pain, and I felt a terrible sadness come over me. A sadness so deep I almost couldn't bear it.

Ain't gonna live to see the new year. The words streamed into my mind one at a time, like little boats set to sail on a river. *Ain't gonna get that crop in at all.* I looked over at him. He was singing "Happy Birthday" and smiling.

Then I could see what he was seeing in his mind: his own birthday in this very schoolhouse seventy years ago. A little boy in britches and suspenders. He was seeing flowers and fish jumping at dusk in the Dog River, and the face of his wife. All the things he was going to miss after they buried him up on Cutler's Hill. I could see that too. That's where they'd bury him. Right next to his mama. There was more, much more, but my head suddenly felt like a sponge too full of water, and then everything went black.

The next thing I knew, I was staring up at the fan on the ceiling of the classroom, and Mrs. Harner, Shawnie and Caleb were bent down over me. When I asked Shawnie what had happened, she wouldn't say. She just shook her head and kept pushing her glasses up and down on her nose.

When I felt well enough to stand, Mrs. Harner asked Caleb to escort me outside.

"How did you know?" he asked as he walked with me over to the well for a drink of water.

"How did I know what?"

"About that old guy. How did you know . . . when he was gonna . . . die?" I looked at Caleb, not wanting to believe what he'd said.

"What happened in there, Caleb? What did I do?" I had a terrible feeling that I'd drooled all over myself or fallen like a lump to the ground, exposing my underwear.

"Well, you sort of got all white and stood real still, like a statue. It didn't even look like you were breathing. You closed your eyes and then in a really calm voice, you said, "You're going to die, Mr. Carver. But not until spring. You'll get your crop in.""

I felt like I might pass out again. "Did everybody hear me?"

"No. Mr. Carver heard you and . . . I heard you. I think everybody else thought you just passed out."

That brought it to a total of four. Fellini, Shawnie, Caleb and Mr. Carver. I could see the list growing daily as my full "abilities" revealed themselves.

"What did Mr. Carver do?"

"He looked like he'd just seen the Ghost of Christmas Future. Turned almost as white as you and excused himself. But he seemed . . . relieved in a way."

I nodded. "Thanks, Caleb," I said, and started walking back to the schoolhouse, but Caleb held on to my arm.

"Are you embarrassed or something?"

"Wouldn't you be?"

"No way. Whatever it was you did in there was great. I don't think you should be embarrassed. I think you're amazing."

"You do?"

"Yeah. I do. But I don't want to know when I'm going to die or anything, so if you get any messages about me, I'd appreciate it if you could keep them to yourself."

I laughed.

"What else can you do, anyway?"

I shook my head. "I don't really know. It keeps changing." I put my hands in the pocket of my skirt, looked down at the ground and kicked the dirt. I didn't want to talk to Caleb about this. I wanted to go back to talking about stars and trees. He seemed to understand, and changed the subject.

"So, is it true what Shawnie says? You're going to be up on that mountain all winter long?"

"The trail to the Hollow is too dangerous in the winter, so I study at home with Felix. I come back to school in April."

"Well, I'm planning to come up for the fair in April. Maybe I could meet you there, if that's all right."

My heart was beating furiously. "That would be fine," I said. "April would be fine."

★

CHAPTER FIVE

★

"HARMONY!" I TRIED pulling myself from the dream but it was too strong. I fell back to sleep.

"Harmony! Throw it! Throw it over here!" Shawnie was screaming at me from the outfield, which was gold and red and full of late-afternoon light.

"Harmony!" I looked at the white ball in my hand. A name was scrawled in red ink across the hide. I stared at the name, but couldn't make out what it said. I pulled my arm back, opened my fist and let go. The white ball sailed forward like a rocket, hitting Caleb hard on the side of the head, knocking him into a pile of leaves.

"Harmony!"

"I'm sorry!" I yelled. "I didn't mean to. I'm sorry."
Caleb sat up and winked at me. He held the ball up over
his head and said something that sounded like "mush-
rooms" or "love you" or "bush moon." I couldn't hear
him clearly.

"What?" I asked. Caleb shook his head and smiled.

"You did it again. You're amazing." A warmth spread
through my body and a hand touched my shoulder.

★   ★   ★

"Harmony!"

I rolled over.

"Wake up, honey. Ten past eight. Chickens are
fussin'." I opened my eyes, squinting into the cold blue
winter light of my bedroom.

"Nettie Mae?"

"Who'd you expect? The Queen of Sheba?" She
touched the inside of her wrist to my forehead. "Warm,
but not hot." Why was everyone forever checking me
for fever?

"I feel fine." I brushed her hand away. "I was just
dreaming," I said irritably, wishing I could go back to
the ball field with Caleb.

"Sleeping like a coon dog at noon," Nettie Mae
said, pulling back the curtains. "Not healthy to stay in
bed past sunrise. Missing the best part of the day."

"I'm growing, Nettie Mae," I said, sitting up and
pulling the covers around me.

"A person can grow just as well out of bed as in it,"
she said, closing the door behind her.

I *have* been sleeping later than usual and dreaming more . . . about Caleb. I miss him. I miss Shawnie, too. Every week she sends me a letter with the latest updates as to my condition. I know more now about psychic phenomena and telekinesis than I'd ever want to know. I can see Shawnie poring over her medical books, seeking to define me. But I don't really care if what I am has a name. I'd just like to enjoy it a little more.

Last Saturday night, I spent the whole evening in my room thinking about Caleb and flipping dimes on my bedspread by staring at Franklin Roosevelt's forehead. I even practiced changing the stations on the radio without touching the dial. And after Nettie Mae and Felix went to bed, I tiptoed into the kitchen to make myself a sandwich and rearrange the silverware. It's probably not how most people spend their Saturday nights, but it made me happy.

Even though I told Shawnie I thought my new abilities would go away, I hope they don't. At least not the feeling of them—that amazing electricity just before the spoons move or the radio dial shifts or the smoke alarms go off. If I could keep it quiet and learn how to control it, I'd like to have that feeling every moment of my life.

I feel it most strongly when I'm out in the woods, away from everything and everyone. Compared to chickadees surviving the winter and giant maple trees growing from one tiny seed, anything I can do seems quite ordinary. I wouldn't mind if the whole forest knew about what I could do. Trees don't need anything from me; they have no reason to make a fuss. In the world of human beings, though, I'm afraid the more of them who know, the less the gift will be truly mine.

One night after a snowstorm, I pulled myself high up into the branches of Nula with the rope Felix and I had rigged up, and sat in the alcove her lower branches make, like a little seat. I sat there with Nula's strong trunk supporting me and listened to the branches of smaller trees snap under the weight of the snow. Each snap sent an echo into the woods, like footsteps. Nettie Mae says it is Ogilo, the winter sister, out collecting firewood to tide her over until spring.

As I lay there with my head against Nula's sweet-smelling bark, watching the snow fall onto my mittens, I felt it. It was so clear, so strong. I could feel everything around me and inside me at the same time. All of it— Nula, the air against my face, the Cherokee spirits just beyond the trees, the stars above me and the darkness. It was all alive, nothing separating any of it. I knew then that if anything happened to me or Nula or the stars, everything would feel it—everything.

"Harmony! Those chickens are going to eat their own eggs for breakfast if you don't get out there," Nettie Mae called from the kitchen.

"I'm coming," I yelled, pulling away from my thoughts. I swung my legs over the side of the bed and reached for my slippers, trying to keep my feet at least an inch above the floor. In the winter all the floors in our house are like ice. Felix always means to give us a proper floor before the first snow, but so far there never ends up being anything more between our bare feet and the cold ground than one thin layer of plywood.

"In Burma," Felix says, "there isn't even plywood."

"In Burma," I remind him, "there isn't any snow."

Felix laughs and shrugs. "I'll get to it, darlin'. One of these days. Don't you fret."

"You better make haste. Felix has his maps spread out," Nettie Mae said, poking her head in and rolling her eyes.

★   ★   ★

In the winter months, I study at home with Felix. We spend our mornings looking at maps of the world. For the past month we've been studying Tibet, Bhutan and Burma—all places we want to go one day. Nettie Mae says Burma sounds like a perfect place for Felix and me—Burma or Timbuktu. To Nettie Mae, it's all the same. She can't understand why anyone would want to see the world, when the world is always right where you are anyway.

Our afternoons are usually spent studying philosophy, astronomy and Felix's idea-of-the-month. This month it's free energy. Which, from what I can understand, has to do with gathering up the energy that swirls around us all the time, but that we can't see. The ether, Felix calls it. He believes it's possible to harness that energy so folks can use it to heat their homes and cook their food without using up oil, cutting down trees and generally destroying the earth, which sounds like a good idea to me.

Lately, though, our afternoons are filled with plans to save the Old People. Felix doesn't want Nettie Mae fretting over the subject. He says she's too emotionally involved to be of any help anyway, and I must agree. Whenever the subject comes up, which it does every evening at dinner, her face twists up in worry and she starts talking about tying herself to trees or lying down in front of bulldozers, if she has to. Felix knows that's exactly what she'd do, if given the chance, so he is developing a more organized and rational plan that doesn't involve anyone throwing themselves in front of heavy machinery. He explained the whole thing to me the other night after Nettie Mae went to bed.

"There are six Old People, Harmony," he told me. "And you and I are going to build platforms up in their branches and ask Asa Bowen, Jeb Hawkins, Hyde Fister, Jonathan Back and McAllister Brown to sit in the trees with us when the lumbermen come. The Old People are so close together that no one could cut one without it falling into another, and if there are live folks up there, why, then they couldn't cut them down at all. We might not be able to hold them off forever, but it'll give us some time to implement Plan B." Felix smiled. He wouldn't go into the details of Plan B with me yet, but knowing Felix, it's probably elaborate and followed closely by Plans C and D, and maybe even E.

Whatever plan Felix decides on is fine with me. Even though I have no idea how to build a platform or hold off a bunch of angry loggers by sitting on one, I'll do my best. I'll keep this secret with Felix if it will help save the trees and keep Nettie Mae from worry.

★

CHAPTER SIX

★

"LET'S BE ON our way, Harmony," Nettie Mae called to me, then whistled for Wilson. Every Thursday Nettie Mae makes her rounds, and she likes me to go with her. We walk the long trail up into the mountains, pulling Anthony behind us. He is loaded down with buttonberry preserves, blankets, baked ham, chicken pies and Nettie Mae's medicine bundle, passed down to her from her great-grandmother Twila, a Cherokee healer. The bundle is two feet long and two feet wide, swaddled up in leather. It is tied with a braided piece of horsehair with several chipped beads hanging from the end. I don't know all the contents of the bundle, as I have never been sick enough for Nettie Mae to use them on me. But I know it contains strange roots and oils. When the bundle starts getting thin and she needs to restock the contents, she'll take it far out in the woods to a special place she has and make it fat again.

There is only one person right now who Nettie Mae uses the bundle for: old Willa Henshaw, whose cabin sits on the edge of Harriman Ravine. It's a good thing Willa isn't a sleepwalker, because if she were to walk out her front door and turn left instead of right, she'd end up at the bottom of that ravine in less than a minute, and no one could ever get to her down there. But falling down the ravine is something Willa doesn't have to trouble herself about anymore, because she never leaves her house. She rarely leaves her bed.

Willa is dying.

Nettie Mae says it's a natural thing to die, nothing to be afraid of, but I don't like all the time Nettie Mae spends with Willa while she's doing it. Some days when Nettie Mae comes home, I can smell Willa on her and it's like the smell of leaves rotting away into the earth.

After my encounter with Mr. Carver in the fall, I'm afraid of what I might hear or feel when I'm with Willa. I can usually find a good excuse not to go with Nettie Mae on Thursdays. I suddenly will decide to clean my room or help Felix with a new project. But Felix wanted time to himself today to compose a letter to Burston Jones and the Great Northern Lumber Company about what's taking them so long to cut down our trees. And he was sending me on a mission to deliver notes to Jonathan Back and McAllister Brown about our plan.

I pulled my wool sweater around me and grabbed a hat. This morning Felix said he could smell spring on the wind, but I think it'll still be a few weeks before the crocuses by the back door poke their heads out. I think they are the bravest of all flowers, crocuses. Felix calls them little pirates, stealing the first rays of the spring sun all for themselves.

As I came down the porch steps, I almost collided with Wilson as he tore around the corner of the house chasing a chipmunk. Wilson is part hound, part collie. He's got the nose of a hound and the timid nature of a collie. Scared to death of anything larger than a squirrel, Wilson will track a fox for ten miles with his nose and when he finally trees it, he'll sit at the bottom and whine and bawl, hoping the fox won't come down. If it threatens to, Wilson runs off with his tail between his legs. Felix says Wilson is like a lot of men. He likes the chase, but when he gets close to the real thing, he's too afraid to reach out and grab it.

"Give it up, Wilson," I called after him.

"Come along!" Nettie Mae yelled. "I swear, the two of you are slower than molasses in January." She had Anthony by the rope and was starting up the trail without us. Wilson and I ran to catch up.

It takes forty minutes of walking straight uphill to reach Jonathan and Sila Back's place. That's Nettie

Mae's first stop. They have a brand-new baby girl named Greta Jane Back, born one week ago on a windy Wednesday night. No one in these parts has a telephone, but Nettie Mae has been delivering babies so long, she doesn't need a phone to know when they're coming. So far she hasn't missed one.

"Hey there, Nettie Mae." Sila greeted us at the cabin door with Greta in her arms. I hadn't seen Sila since her belly was big and full, and she looked real different. Slim again and soft, like she'd just bathed in milk for a week, all pink and glowing. Nettie Mae calls that the afterglow. It's a good sign.

"Come on inside." Sila opened the door for us.

"If you don't mind, Sila, I'd like to rest out here in the fresh air for a spell and catch my breath." Nettie Mae gets winded on the walk up the mountain these days. Felix and I think she should ride on Anthony, but she won't hear of it. "Folks will think I've gotten lazy. When I can no longer walk my rounds, that'll be the day I stop."

"I'll bring you some hot cider," Sila said softly. "Jonathan's gone down to the Hollow for supplies; he'll be home soon." Sila gestured with a slender arm in the direction of the side porch. "Won't you sit?"

"Thank you, Sila." Nettie Mae walked over and lowered herself into the porch rocker. "Let me see that fine child." She reached out her strong hands and Sila gladly passed the baby into them, then disappeared into the house.

"Healthy baby girl! Look at her, Harmony." I touched the baby's nose with the tip of my finger.

"She's a strong one, Sila," Nettie Mae called in through the screen door. "She's a Back through and through, tightly muscled and fierce." Nettie Mae delivered Jonathan twenty years ago. She says all the Backs are strong as oxen. They could put in a full day's work and then dance from midnight till dawn, even into their eighties.

"It's the mountain air," Nettie Mae said, leaning close to me and cuddling the little girl. "Mountain air makes babies strong. Just like you."

I don't ordinarily think of myself as strong. Felix says I'm kind of slight and airy, and maybe he's right. Looking at me, "strong" would probably not be the first word to pop into someone's head. But Nettie Mae may have a point too. I can haul water from the well to the house without having to stop and rest, and I can get Anthony going when he gets stubborn and digs his heels into the mud by pulling hard on his tether. And as a newborn, I must have lain out for some time in that crisp mountain air with no clothes on before Felix found me.

There are all kinds of theories about how I arrived on this mountain, and each person strongly promotes their own version. Some say that since Nettie Mae is a midwife, it makes sense that some poor young woman would have left me at her doorstep. But other mountain folk like a good mystery, and believe I was spirited here on the wind or left behind by the ghost of a Cherokee maiden. Dilly Topham read my palm once and told me she couldn't get a clear image of my birthplace. "Just a swirling mass of colored clouds" was what she told me, which goes along perfectly with Felix's version. Nettie Mae has never given her opinion on the matter, and no one has ever asked me what I think. Maybe it's a good thing, since I'm not sure myself.

If I had to pick one story, though, I guess I'd prefer the mystery. It would explain a lot about my new abilities and also cast out the possibility that I was merely left out in the cold with no clothes on by someone who didn't want me. I'm not as lucky as Greta Back—knowing from the very beginning where I came from and who I belong to.

Sometimes I have dreams that I'm traveling through a tunnel of wind so fast I can't see anything. I'll spin like crazy and then when I think I can't go any faster, I'll fall. But before I hit the ground, something catches me and I wake up. It's more like a memory than a dream, really. A very old memory.

★   ★   ★

"I'm afraid all I've got is a bit of sun tea, will that do?" Sila asked as she pushed through the porch door with two Mason jars in her hand.

"It'll do fine," Nettie Mae said, reaching out and taking one jar from Sila's hand. I took the other.

"Now sit yourself down and rest, honey. No more waiting on us. Harmony can do some fetching."

Nettie Mae and Sila started talking about babies and I wandered into the kitchen to get Nettie Mae an extra blanket to wrap Greta in.

The inside of Sila's house was warm and smelled like wood smoke and the sweet powdery scent of a baby. Sila had all Greta's tiny undershirts and diapers laid out on a small wooden dresser. A picture of Sila's mama sat to one side.

I love to wander around a house when I'm the only one inside it. I like to take in the feeling of a place. I've been inside many houses with Nettie Mae. Some are cold and stiff around the edges, and some are so full of sorrow it's hard to breathe inside them, but the Backs' house bursts with possibility. Lace curtains at the windows, a pair of red socks folded neatly on the sideboard and a small pot of honey on the kitchen table.

★ ★ ★

A light caught my eye. A clear crystal hanging from the kitchen window swung a little from a draft. The sun reflected off its sharp angles, making it shine. I walked over and stared at it, and that familiar, tingling feeling traveled down my arms. I felt slightly electric, and I couldn't take my eyes off the crystal. It moved back and forth, sending sparks of light all around the kitchen.

I could feel the crystal. I could feel something that was inside it. Something alive. I knew if I asked the crystal to move, it would. So I did. I asked it to spin in a circle, and it spun.

I moved around the kitchen, keeping my eyes on the

crystal as it spun on its own. The light from the window sent a beam across my shirt, and for a moment it felt like the whole room and everything in it was glowing.

"We're ready for those blankets, Harmony," Nettie Mae called from the porch.

"Yes, ma'am." I stopped in front of the crystal, reached out and put my fingers around it. It was warm and I could feel a slight vibration, like a hum in my fingers, and then it was gone. I let it go and it swung gently, then stopped. My hands were shaking a little, but I turned from the window and grabbed two small, soft blankets from the top of the bureau behind me and headed back outside.

The air had turned colder since we'd arrived, and the wind was up. Nettie Mae held Greta close to her. She reached out and took both blankets and quickly swaddled Greta's tiny body in them, so all that could be seen of her was a pink face and a mass of dark hair.

"Reminds me of Harmony. She was this age when she came to us."

"I remember," Sila said. "I was only ten at the time, but my mama used to tell me the story every night before I went to bed. For a long time I thought she'd just made it up."

"True as true can be," Nettie Mae said. Then she started into the details of how Felix found me, and my mind began to drift back to the crystal. I've heard the story so many times and even though Nettie Mae changes some of the details so as not to bore me, I'd be happy never to hear it told again. But folks up here like to hear it over and over and when Nettie Mae is done telling it, they just sit back and sigh and say things like "My, my, can you believe anything like that?" or "Golly, what a story," and slap their knees as if Nettie Mae had just told them for the first time instead of the twentieth.

I smiled and nodded when Nettie Mae or Sila mentioned my name, but my mind wasn't with them. I was thinking about the crystal. I wanted to go home and hang one of Felix's crystals on a string and practice with it for the rest of the day.

After a little while, Nettie Mae whistled for Wilson and motioned for me to join her. But we weren't going home. We were going farther up the mountain. I handed Felix's note to Sila and asked her to give it to Jonathan.

"It's about the Old People," I told her.

"I'll be sure he gets it," Sila said, folding the note into her pocket.

★   ★   ★

Nettie Mae pulled herself out of the porch chair and gave Greta back to her mama, then asked me to fetch Anthony for her. I hugged Sila, gave Greta a kiss on her tiny forehead and walked out into the yard to unhitch the mule from a pine tree. It was close to noon and it was beginning to rain. We pulled ponchos on and headed up the mountain.

★

CHAPTER
SEVEN

★

WILLA HENSHAW IS the great-granddaughter of Samuel
Henshaw, the first white settler in these parts. He
started the lumber mill and the general store, and hired
a minister to come in and give services in the little
church in Gospel Hollow once a month. Nettie Mae
said he was known for being stern and silent and I can
imagine it, because his great-granddaughter is not
much different. Nettie Mae has been taking me to visit
Willa Henshaw since I could walk, and I've never enjoyed a single visit. Not ever. She used to make me cry
when I was little. That's what I remember most. I'd sit
in the wrong place on the sofa or fidget with some

knickknack on a shelf and she'd say, "Nettie Mae, that child is a bundle of trouble. Sit her out on the porch so I don't have to look at her." Nettie Mae would explain to Willa that it was perfectly natural for a child my age to fidget. Then she'd hug me while I cried, wrap me tight in a blanket and set me out on the porch with a cup of warm milk and a pretty picture book. It was a relief to sit outside and get out from the dark, stuffy rooms of Willa's cabin and replace the ugly picture of Willa's face with beautiful pictures in a book.

Nettie Mae was tending Willa way back then, and she's still doing it. Though now Willa doesn't have some made-up illness like she used to, when she would ask Nettie Mae to bundle up her corns or tend to her stiff joints. Nettie Mae says Willa has got something for sure now, 'cause all her energy is draining away.

"Why do you bring me up here to see Willa, anyway?" I asked Nettie Mae as we pulled Anthony behind us in the rain. "She's so miserable and I'm always tired after we leave." These were the moments I wished I were back at school with Shawnie instead of stuck up on the mountain. Sometimes April seemed a long way off.

"Harmony, I bring you here so you can see the worst of it. Willa is about the toughest person I know. My grandmother told me that if you can find love for the hardest folks, then you can find it for yourself. Willa is my teacher. She teaches me patience."

Halfway up the path to Willa's we came upon the cairn, a small pile of rocks shaped like a witch's hat.

This is the point where the path diverges. Straight on, it leads to Willa's cliff and the ravine below. To the right, it winds and twists through ferns and brambles down to McAllister Brown's cabin. Once I dreamt of the cairn. I was walking up this path after the first snowfall, and when I reached the pile of rocks, it turned into a dragon and chased me back down the path, melting the snow behind me, breathing fire down my neck. At the bottom of the path was Felix all dressed in white, holding a map of the world in his hands. He threw a bucket of water on me and I woke up.

" 'Two roads diverged in a wood, and I—I took the one less traveled by, and that has made all the difference.' " Nettie Mae recites the quote from Robert Frost whenever we reach this point and looks directly at me, which I find rather curious. I'll be glad one day when there is no longer a need to take the less traveled path. We usually have to cut through a week's worth of vines and brush in the summer to get up to Willa's because no one but McAllister checks in on her. Now in early spring, the trail is muddy but clear, lined with bright green ferns just beginning to unfurl.

Outside Willa's cabin, I tied Anthony to a tree and took out two metal bowls—one for Anthony and one for Wilson. I walked over to the open well and drew up a bucket. The only thing I liked about Willa's place was the view. On a clear day you could see practically all the way to Knoxville.

"Nettie Mae, is that you out there? What took you

so long? Don't you care that I'm dying?" Willa's raspy voice echoed out to the yard, followed by a long, loose, hacking cough. "Is the girl with you?"

I looked over at Nettie Mae and she gave me a smile. She mouthed the word "teacher" to me and I rolled my eyes.

Nettie Mae went inside while I enjoyed the fresh air for a few more minutes, slowly unpacking the extra blankets and food Nettie Mae had brought, and combing down Anthony. I've never considered myself a timid person. But I have to admit that Willa is the one person who can get under my skin.

"I don't want to go in there to see that miserable old witch," I whispered in Anthony's big, fleshy ear.

"Harmony?" Nettie Mae called. "Bring in the food now."

"Wish I were a mule like you, Anthony." Anthony shook his head and lowered it for more water.

The stale air of the cabin hit my nose as I walked in and for a moment, I felt like I couldn't breathe. My heart started racing. The air felt like it was stuck and confused and couldn't figure out how to move around anymore or make its way out the door. That's what Willa's presence did to me.

I walked slowly toward the bedroom, across the kitchen with its small window on one wall, the sill lined with tiny ceramic dogs. All the shades in the house were drawn, so only a few random cracks of light could seep in. The whole place smelled of liniment. I stood in the doorway of the bedroom and waited for Nettie Mae to turn around. Willa was sitting up in bed in a white cotton nightgown. I've always thought Willa resembled a bird of prey: piercing eagle eyes, sharp cheekbones and jet-black hair streaked with white. I made a shiny shell over my heart as I stood in the doorway, preparing myself for Willa's unkind words. Nettie Mae sat in a straight-back chair next to the bed, holding one of Willa's clawlike hands and checking her pulse.

"Well, I'm still alive, if that's what you're checking for," Willa barked.

"Oh, I know that," Nettie Mae said kindly. "I'm just checking to see how glad you are to see me today, Willa."

"Well, I'm not glad. Damn it. I've been waiting all week. You said you'd be here first thing. First thing in the morning, you told me, and it's nearly noon."

"Did I?" said Nettie Mae, looking wistfully out the window. "Well, I'm sorry, Willa, I don't recall saying that. Harmony and I had to stop up and see the new Back baby, and it was hard to tear ourselves away from that sweet thing."

"Babies." Willa turned her head as if she might let out another horrid cough, but no sound came. "I suppose it's ugly. All babies are ugly."

"It was beautiful," I said. "She was beautiful. And she smelled all sweet and new." I just couldn't let Willa have her last miserable word on everything.

Willa grunted and looked over in my direction.

Willa has a way of looking right through a person and out the other side and never seeming pleased with what she sees. "You've gotten right skinny over the winter." Willa threw the words at me and they bounced right off my shiny shell and fell to the floor.

"You've gotten skinny too," I said.

"I have a good reason and don't you sass me, girl. She's always been bold, hasn't she, Nettie Mae?"

"Well, I don't know about that. She's a fine girl. A good help to me and Felix. And she loves babies." Nettie Mae winked at me.

"Babies," Willa sighed. "Can't stand the crying, the mess, the general nuisance."

"Well, now how would you ever know?" Nettie Mae said. "You never did have one, did you? Unless I missed something." Willa's eyes narrowed in Nettie Mae's direction.

"That'll be enough, Nettie Mae."

"All right," Nettie Mae said lightly. "Harmony and I brought you some delicious food, didn't we, Harmony?"

"Yes, ma'am," I said, looking at the floor. *The old witch doesn't deserve anything nice*, I thought. But I unpacked the satchel and laid the loaf of bread and a chicken pie on the bed.

"Not in here, girl!" Willa shrieked. "Not on the bed. You'll make a mess."

"I will *not* make a mess," I answered back, full of spit.

"Off the bed, off the bed!" she screeched, reaching for me with her claw hand. Little bumps rose up on the skin of my arms and I pulled as far away from her as possible. I didn't want her to touch me.

"All right," I said over her screech. "I'll put it all away." My voice was shaky. I started gathering up the food, glad of an excuse to leave.

"Get out! Get out!" Her words were like someone slapping me across the face.

"I'm getting out!" My voice rose to meet hers. "I'm getting out, you ungrateful old—"

"Harmony!" Nettie Mae stopped me before a flood of words poured forth. She gave me a stern look. "You go on, now. I'll be finished in a minute. Go on." I left the food where it was and walked out of the bedroom. Behind me, I could hear the soothing tone of Nettie Mae's voice. The same voice she used with babies and animals that were afraid.

I ran out into the yard and over to Anthony.

"Why do I come here, Anthony? Why do I let her get to me? An old dying woman like that." Anthony swung his head back and forth as if to say he had no idea why human beings did what they did.

"Well, what was that all about?" Nettie Mae stood on the porch with her hands on her hips, but I could see she was holding back a smile.

"I'm sorry, Nettie Mae," I said, walking toward her. "That woman just riles me. I feel like I can't breathe when I'm in the same room with her."

"I know, honey," Nettie Mae said, sitting down on the porch steps. "I can't blame you. She's as ornery as a skunk."

"Why?" I asked. "What makes her so mean?"

Nettie Mae considered my question for a moment. "Well, Willa's daddy was very strict with her when she was young. She had a beautiful voice—a natural-born gift, but her daddy forbade her to sing. No one knows why. He was such a strange, hard man. Willa wasn't strong enough to stand up to him, she was so young. She stopped singing—kind of dried up inside because she couldn't let her gift out into the world." Nettie Mae shook her head. "That's a sad thing to keep all that beauty inside. She's been full of bitter words ever since."

"What do you do, Nettie Mae, when those words come flying at you? I've tried giving myself a hard shell that her words can't seep into like they do my skin, but it doesn't always work."

Nettie Mae gestured for me to sit down beside her, and put her hand on my shoulder. "Making a shell isn't the answer, honey. Shells just get tougher and tougher until you don't let anything in. You think a shell will protect you from pain, but what it ends up doing is keeping all the pain inside."

"What can I do, Nettie Mae? She's the only person I've ever been afraid of."

"You have to do something that seems real backwards at first, honey. You have to take her words in deep and feel them. Let the pain of them swirl around inside you. Feel how they hurt you and then wish yourself peace. If you ask the pain in, there's no longer reason to fear it and no reason to build a shell to keep it out. After a while, you'll feel your heart relax. Then maybe one day you can wish Willa peace. Lord knows she could use some."

"Where in tarnation have you got to? Are you both crazy?" Willa's words came right at me. I took a deep breath and tried to let them in, but it felt hard to do.

"I'll try, Nettie Mae," I said. "But I won't make any promises."

Nettie Mae smiled. "Maybe you can stay out here and keep Anthony company and round up Wilson." She moved toward the door. "We'll be on our way soon." She gave me a wink and I knew she was releasing me from any further torture.

★   ★   ★

McAllister Brown lives half a mile from Willa Henshaw. He checks in on her in the cool weather to make sure her fire is lit and she has a hot meal when she's hungry. Nettie Mae can't get there every day, so McAllister does what he can.

We walked in silence the whole way, both of us deep in thought—me about losing my temper with Willa, and Nettie Mae most likely working out a new tincture she was planning to give McAllister for his gout.

They say that gout is a disease of kings—men who consume rich food and don't get much exercise—but nothing could be further from the truth in McAllister's case. More than eighty years old, tall and lean as a stick, McAllister chops wood and plows his small rocky fields from sunup till sundown. "It simply runs in his family," Nettie Mae told me as we climbed the little rise and looked down upon his cabin. "And he doesn't sit still long enough to give it any attention. If he'd only do as I say and stay off that foot for a week, he'd be cured." Neither of us can imagine McAllister sitting still for longer than fifteen minutes, though, except when he's asleep.

McAllister greeted us halfway down the path. "Thought I'd have visitors soon. Heard Willa screeching. Figured you stopped to check her. Saw her yesterday. Brought her some kale from my garden. Told me to get my muddy boots off her clean floor. Said soon enough I'd be able to walk over her grave in them. No need to rush things. Screeched like a hoot owl. Threw a pillow at me."

That's how McAllister usually talks—short little sentences, like some kind of secret code. He chuckled. "Hard to believe anyone with so much fire in 'em could be so close to dying."

"It's my experience that folks die the way they live, and Willa is no exception," Nettie Mae said matter-of-factly.

McAllister nodded and pulled a homemade cigarette from his pocket. "Could be right. Could be right," he said softly, considering Nettie Mae's words and lighting up.

"Why don't you ladies come in? Sit for a spell. Nettie, you can give this old foot a look-see." Nettie Mae nodded. I grabbed a parcel of food, and we both ducked inside.

McAllister's cabin looks a lot like him: spare, dirty and a little rumpled around the edges, but warm, too. The exact opposite of Willa's. He scurried into the kitchen, limping a little, and came back with a pan of fried corn bread and a sweet for me. He makes his own taffy twice a year and keeps a stash for whenever I come. Taffy isn't my favorite candy, but I took it gratefully and put it in my pocket for later. Felix loves McAllister's taffy, so I save it for him. McAllister might be a little rough and smelly, but he *is* kind.

Nettie Mae gave McAllister a good long looking-over, then offered him her usual piece of advice. "McAllister, you'll probably live a whole heap longer than I will, so I don't have much right to tell you what to do." Nettie Mae knows how to sweet-talk the older men, get their pride up so they'll listen. "But if you don't care for this foot, you'll be spending those years in pain or in bed, and I don't think that's what you want, is it?"

"No, ma'am. It isn't," McAllister said, rubbing at his kneecap. "But this land is all I got and I'm all it's got. Can't just sit on my duff watching the weeds grow. Now can I?"

"One week, McAllister. That's all it'll take. Not that many weeds can grow in a week. Stay off it for seven days or until the swelling goes down, and then take the medicine I brought. Every day for a month, you hear?"

A smile cracked McAllister's thin lips. "You have a way, Nettie, now don't you? Always have. Why, Harmony, I remember when this old gal was the prettiest young thing in these parts. Course I was too old at the time to take advantage of such beauty, but there were others who didn't let the chance slip by, if I remember correctly." McAllister winked at me. "What men will do for a beautiful woman." McAllister sighed and Nettie Mae rolled her eyes.

"McAllister, maybe I better give you some medicine for your memory. I think you were remembering someone else."

"No, ma'am. I was remembering you. Pretty, just like this young'un here." I felt myself blush.

"Hold still, now, McAllister," Nettie Mae said as she ran her fingers over his big toe one last time. She studied it for a few minutes, then turned and reached into one of her bags. "All right, you can put your sock back on." McAllister took his foot off the stool it was perched on and pulled a red wool sock over his toes. The sock looked like it had been darned so many times that the darning was all that was holding it together. There didn't appear to be very much actual sock left. Nettie Mae held a little brown glass bottle up to the fading light and handed it to McAllister. "That was a long time ago," she said quietly.

I've seen pictures of Nettie Mae when she was

young and I know McAllister is almost right. Except I wouldn't say she was pretty—I'd say she was beautiful. Sometimes I'll come across an old photo of Nettie Mae and it's hard to believe the girl with the long dark hair and sweet face could possibly be the same woman I know. Nettie Mae is only sixty-four years old, but she looks a lot older. Life on the mountain can be hard.

The sun was beginning to make its descent in the sky. I slipped Felix's note into McAllister's hand and gave him a wink so he wouldn't say anything. He nodded to me and tucked it into the cuff of his sleeve. Nettie Mae and I gathered our things and said goodbye for another week. McAllister pulled a wool sweater around his chest and, folding his arms over it, walked us out into the yard. "Best be gettin' on before the sky opens. It'll be a cold rain." Nettie Mae looked up at the blue-black clouds and whistled for Wilson.

"It's time we were heading home, Harmony."

★

CHAPTER
EIGHT

★

"So how's the old witch?" Felix asked with a chuckle
as he helped Nettie Mae and me take off our slickers.
The sky *had* opened up on us halfway down the mountain just like McAllister had said it would, and it had
been a long, soggy journey to our front door.

"Did she die yet?"

"Felix McGillicuddy! I think it is truly unkind to
make light of a person's final days."

Felix winked at Nettie Mae. "Now, you know I
don't mean no harm, darlin'. It's just that she's been
dying for twenty years. It's the longest dying I ever
heard of."

"Well, she's really doing it this time. She looks like a scarecrow—all skin and bones. Not much interest in food, and I think she's losing her desire to drink."

"She can still screech, though," I said.

"I'll bet she can." Felix laughed. He raised his right eyebrow to me, his way of asking if I'd accomplished my mission. I gave him a thumbs-up and he smiled.

"Sit down, darlin'," he said, pulling up a chair for Nettie Mae. "You look mighty tuckered." He patted Nettie Mae gently on the shoulder, and Nettie Mae held on to his hand and kissed the back of it.

"Felix, you are a fine sight on a stormy night."

"Some good hot food will fix you right up," he said, rubbing the back of her neck.

Felix made us a dinner of corn chowder and home-made bread. He usually lets Nettie Mae do the cooking, but on occasion he can whip up a fine feast.

Felix served up supper and we ate silently until the edge was taken off our hunger. Then he leaned back a ways in his chair, folded his napkin a couple of times and cleared his throat.

"Saturday is the Huntsville Fair," he announced in a hopeful way.

"That's nice," Nettie Mae replied between mouth-fuls of soup.

"Well, honey, I thought this year we should go."

Nettie Mae was silent.

Every spring Felix talks about going to the Huntsville Fair, but Nettie Mae always says no. They have only been once—twenty-two years ago. It's where they met for the first time and even though Huntsville is only sixty miles from our house, they've never been back. Nettie Mae says she wants to keep the memory of their first meeting pure.

Over the years we've heard that the Huntsville Fair has acquired a midway with Ferris wheels and a loop-the-loop roller coaster shaped like a giant centipede. I think it sounds wonderful. The only fair I've ever been to is the one at Hildeen. It's a country fair with cows and chickens and half a dozen rides for little kids. Shawnie goes to Huntsville every spring with her family, and from what she's told me I know it's a lot bigger and more fun than anywhere I've ever been. But the real reason I want to go this year is to see Caleb.

Nettie Mae says the Huntsville Fair is not the same now that it's so big. Twenty-two years ago, the only ride was an old merry-go-round with seventeen horses. Nettie Mae and Felix rode on the back of a glossy black stallion all night until the man who ran the merry-go-round had to go home to bed.

"Yes, sir. We got our money's worth that night, didn't we, honey?" Felix will say, giving her a kiss on the cheek.

Nettie Mae will nod and smile to herself. "Yes, we certainly did, Felix."

"Why don't we go to the fair this year, Nettie Mae?" I pleaded. "I hear they might not do it next year because of the expense."

"Why, I heard that too. It might be our last chance,

honey, and Harmony has never been. Doesn't seem right to deprive a young'un of going to a fair."

"This sounds like a conspiracy to me," Nettie Mae said, looking from Felix to me and giving us a tired smile. "Well, I'll consider it," she said as she slowly buttered a piece of bread. "But I can't go if Willa is near to passing. And what about the trees?"

"Honey, that woman has been near to passing since I first met her twenty years ago, and we can take a day off from our plans. We have plenty of time. We're making good progress," he said, winking at me.

Felix is in the process of convincing Burston Jones and the Great Northern Lumber Company that we don't care about the mess they want to make of our land. "Come on down," Felix wrote to them. "We're sick to death of having all these trees around us. We could do with some more light."

Felix says he'll let us know when the men from GNL will be coming to help us out. That is how he refers to the Great Northern Lumber Company. GNL. Nettie Mae says it more likely stands for Good for Nothing Louts, but Felix says she has to keep her opinions to herself for now.

"Yep, Felix," she said, smiling from ear to ear. "I think we can get away for one day without the world falling apart."

★

CHAPTER
NINE

★

THE HUNTSVILLE FAIRGROUND is on the outskirts of
Carson City. It sits in a big open field that's used for car
shows and 4-H fairs the rest of the year. Felix, Nettie
Mae and I drove in from the north, so we could see the
peaks of the giant white tents before we descended into
the valley.

It took us three hours to start our trip. We had to
feed Anthony and Wilson, and collect the eggs. And for
some strange reason, Nettie Mae insisted on cleaning
the inside of the cabin from top to bottom before we
could leave. When we finished all that, I climbed into
the backseat of the truck and waited, wishing I could

just think Nettie Mae into the front seat and she'd be there, like I can think about spinning crystals and making fire. I tried, but it didn't work.

After waiting for almost an hour, Felix finally started the truck and left it idling while he practically carried Nettie Mae from the house. "Getting you off this mountain, woman, is a feat of heroism," he told her in exasperation as he buckled her in.

As we drove down the mountain, it was clear that spring had arrived. The mountain was coming alive. The little dome-shaped blossoms of the mountain laurel bush by the side of Ellis landing were wide open, and the air was full of birdsong. I left the window open all the way to Carson City so I wouldn't miss a thing.

The sap was running. The streams were melting. Everything was waking up, including me. I was feeling restless. The roads and trails were now clear of ice and the world was opening again. The world of Caleb and Shawnie and school and the fair. In a way, winter had been easy, hidden away up on the mountain—easy to keep a secret from only two people, instead of the whole world.

Felix parked the truck in the shade of a big old elm tree at the edge of the fairgrounds. It cost $12.60 for all three of us to get in, which Nettie Mae calculated to be fourteen dozen eggs she'd have to sell at the general store in the Hollow before the end of the month. But Felix said not to worry. He'd dipped into his rainy day account for the occasion so it wouldn't set us back a pinch.

I'd never been anyplace like it before. Walking through the archway out front seemed like moving in a dream. A banner made of gold waved the words HUNTSVILLE FAIR into the breeze. It was just like Shawnie had said it would be—hundreds of people, all different shapes and sizes. Everywhere you looked, something was turning or spinning. The smells of popcorn, fried onions and diesel fuel all mixed together in the warm spring air. It was the smell of the world outside the mountains.

I walked a little behind Felix and Nettie Mae, scanning the crowd for Caleb's dark curly hair and trying to keep up with them at the same time. Felix is the type to wander around all day, sampling a little bit of everything until he is satisfied. But Nettie Mae had only one thing on her mind. She walked straight ahead, searching for the merry-go-round, her shoulders stiff and determined.

We found it—way over at the edge of the fairgrounds, next to a chain-link fence and a few kiddie rides. I didn't think it was the same merry-go-round that was here all those years ago. It looked new, and a few of the little open carriages were painted fluorescent green. The music sounded like something I'd heard on Shawnie's CD player. A heavy beat and a woman wailing "Confusion . . ." over and over again. I looked over at Felix and Nettie Mae, thinking they'd be disappointed, but they were both smiling, and they quickly left me behind to buy tickets.

They picked out a big white stallion, as close as they

could come to the black beauty of all those years ago. Felix hoisted Nettie Mae up to ride sidesaddle in front of him. I stood by and waved along with all the mothers who had put children on for the ride. I felt like one of those mothers myself, watching to make sure Nettie Mae and Felix held on tight to the neck of that shiny plastic stallion and didn't fall off.

I watched them for three full rides. Nettie Mae looked so young up on that horse with Felix. Every once in a while she'd lean her head back against Felix's chest and gaze up at the colored banner blowing in the wind at the top of the stallion's pole. Then she'd close her eyes and smile, and so would Felix.

I watched them until I started feeling dizzy, then I looked up and focused my eyes on the giant Centipede roller coaster flying through its loops. It actually did look like a centipede, with all the screaming people waving their arms from the cars. Whenever the Centipede did an upside-down loop, the waving hands became hundreds of squirmy feet—just like when I turn over a rock and the real bug scuttles away into the mud.

It seemed like Nettie Mae and Felix could stay on the merry-go-round forever, and I imagined for a moment that they actually might. I could see them riding around for eternity and never, ever getting dizzy. But I thought if I had to watch one more ride, I'd probably throw up, so I hopped up next to them for a minute as the ride slowed, and we made plans to meet at the picnic grounds for supper.

★   ★   ★

The first place I went to was the House of Mirrors. We have one tiny mirror in our bathroom and I can see only my face in it. Nothing else. I've tried standing on a stool to catch a glimpse of my knees, but it's impossible. I've begun to think of myself as only a face lately. I don't have an accurate picture of my whole self, and I'm curious to see how it's all coming along.

A girl with dark hair and braces waited outside the House of Mirrors. She bought a ticket and stepped inside. I did the same, ducking beneath the heavy canvas flap.

The hall wasn't what I thought it would be. I expected giant plates of glass, but there were just a dozen freestanding mirrors inside one big room. Some made me look like I had a twisted torso and a long, solemn face, and others made my feet as tiny as clamshells and my head as big as a pumpkin. The dark-haired girl and I walked around, trying not to get in each other's way as we laughed at ourselves.

Finally, I reached the regular mirror. It was right before the exit. The dark-haired girl passed it by and left the room, disappearing behind a black velvet curtain. She probably looked at herself in a mirror like that every morning. I wondered if she appreciated how amazing it was to be able to see your head and feet all at the same time.

At first glance I thought the mirror was another trick, an illusion. I stared at my reflection for a long time, trying to take it in. I'd felt things changing inside me and I know I'm a little curvier than I used to be, but the girl looking back at me was pretty, like Nettie Mae says she is. Her eyes seemed brighter, the curve of her face smoother. I turned around and around, taking in the reflection from all angles. As I left the House of Mirrors, I gave her a wink and held myself a little taller.

"Harmony!" Shawnie ran up behind me and grabbed me around the waist, scaring the breath right out of me. "I've been waiting all morning for you. What took you so long?"

"Nettie Mae." I rolled my eyes. "She had to clean the entire house before we left, as if she'll never have another chance."

Shawnie smiled. "My mother is the same way. They can't help it."

We both laughed.

"Hey, thanks for your letters," I said. "They kept me entertained all winter." Shawnie scrunched up her nose.

"Is that all they were to you—entertainment? Did you take any of them seriously? What about the studies they're doing down in Raleigh? They could do tests. Find out everything you're capable of. And what about that woman in Austria—the one who can heal people with her thoughts? You could write to her. If it were me, I'd want to know."

"I appreciate it, Shawnie. I sincerely do. But I don't want to be poked at and tested and put on display for some professors to stare at." Shawnie's face fell. "I'll think about the woman in Austria," I added. Shawnie gave me a skeptical look. "I really will. But today, I just want to have fun. I want to eat cotton candy and ride the Centipede and make believe I'm just like everybody else. Okay?"

She frowned. "Okay. I'll let you off the hook for today."

"Thank you," I said, bowing my head slightly. It was clear that Shawnie had a vision for me I didn't have for myself. It would have been so much better for her to have this gift, instead of me. She'd know exactly what to do with it. She'd share it. She'd help people. Maybe it had been wasted on me. I didn't want to think about it. I didn't want to talk about it. I gazed out over the midway again.

"He's here," Shawnie said.

"Who's here?"

"Harmony McClean! What do you mean *who*? *Who* you've been *thinking* about all winter long, that's *who*. I've never seen him so nervous. Kept checking his hair in the rearview mirror all the way from my house. I don't think he's eaten any solid food since yesterday. I just now convinced him to get a hot dog." She nodded in the direction of a row of concession stands by the midway.

Over the winter months, whenever I thought of Caleb my heart would beat like crazy, and it was doing it again. My knees felt all funny, like they were made of rubber.

Shawnie turned around and spotted him at the same

time I did. He was leaning against a hot dog stand with his back to us. He had a very nice back.

"Caleb!" Shawnie yelled. He turned around and a smile spread across his face when he saw me. I felt like I might pass out. He squirted mustard onto a hot dog, but it missed and landed on his jeans instead. He didn't even notice.

"Where have you been?" Shawnie scolded as he walked over to us. She always seemed a little annoyed and a little glad to see Caleb, like she did with her brothers. She wiped the mustard off his leg with a napkin and shook her head, as if boys were a nuisance you just had to put up with until they grew out of it. Caleb kept his eyes on me the whole time.

"I've been waiting . . . hoping . . . to catch a glimpse of Ms. Harmony McClean here." I looked down at my feet. "I see she finally showed up."

"Just this minute, and she hasn't even been on the Centipede yet, have you?" Shawnie looked at me, and I shook my head.

"Well, then let me be the one to escort you." Caleb extended his arm to me, bowing slightly. I looked over at Shawnie, who was smiling from ear to ear.

"Harmony?" Shawnie said, waiting for my response. I gave her a nod, and the three of us linked arms and headed to the long line for the Centipede.

★

CHAPTER
TEN

★

I RODE ON the Centipede twice and I would have
bought two more tickets, too, only the line was a mile
long. I had the most amazing feeling up there in the sky
with the air rushing through my hair. It was like something I'd felt before, like that old, old memory. It wasn't
exactly like flying—more like being carried through the
air by something bigger than myself. I didn't scream
like everyone else around me. I just closed my eyes and
felt that sweet forward motion, that rise and fall of gravity. It was so familiar, so comfortable, I could have
stayed on the ride all night.

It was the closest I'd ever felt to the wind. It must be

like that for a squirrel high up in a tree—out on the top-most branches when a storm is blowing up. I've often thought of doing just that: climbing out on one of Nula's branches at the very height of a storm, standing up, closing my eyes, feeling the wind blow me around like a leaf.

★   ★   ★

After our last ride on the Centipede, the three of us wandered the midway together eating ice cream and joking around. Shawnie guided us down a narrow alley lined with tents. Sideshows, her favorite. I'd never seen a sideshow before but from the posters outside, I got the general idea. Freaks. That's what people were paying to see.

I wanted to walk by every single sideshow, but Shawnie dragged us into the velvet tent of Talulah, the bearded woman. Sometimes when Shawnie gets an idea in her head, it's hard to say no to her.

Talulah was a tall, slender Cherokee woman standing on a stage displaying herself in a fancy evening gown with a beard streaming down over her bodice. At first, it didn't seem like the beard was real at all, but then a little kid stepped up and gave it a yank. Talulah screamed and her skin got all red where the hair had been pulled, so I knew it wasn't just a disguise.

"See, it's real." Shawnie's eyes lit up. "She suffers from hirsutism. It's a rare hormonal abnormality in women." Caleb and I looked at each other.

I knew Shawnie didn't come to the sideshows simply

to gawk at the misfortunes of others. She wanted to understand them, put a name to what they suffered from so that one day she might be able to help. Shawnie believes that if you can name something, it takes the fear out of it. She's always been that way. One summer, she turned her family's barn into an animal hospital, where she diagnosed and treated everything from porcupines to one-legged frogs. Mrs. Pawlett always wondered where she found them. I think they found *her*.

I appreciated Shawnie's attempt to inform us, but my stomach was beginning to not feel so good, and it wasn't from the rides or the ice cream either. I'd had my fill of sideshows.

Being raised by a Cherokee woman, I've been taught one thing strongly, and that's pride. Not vanity or boastfulness, but respect for yourself. Nettie Mae told me that when the Cherokee were marched out of Tennessee by government soldiers, they did not weep. They held their heads high, carrying their dead in their arms all the way to the treeless land of Oklahoma. "Hold your head high, Harmony," Nettie Mae tells me. I guess Talulah never had anyone like Nettie Mae around to tell her that.

Thankfully it was a short sideshow. After ten minutes of combing and braiding her beard, Talulah finally took a bow and left the small stage while onlookers clapped and filed out of the tent.

The exit of Talulah's tent opened into the entrance of Esmerelda the Fortune-Teller. I tried to walk the other way, but Shawnie nudged me toward it.

"Go on, Harmony. *Ask her about . . . you know . . . your future*," she whispered in my ear. "Caleb and I will wait out here." She tucked a roll of orange tickets into my hand. I looked back at Caleb and he nodded.

"Go ahead. We'll wait. I'll go get us something to drink."

"Okay," I said. I lifted the velvet doorway into the tent. I didn't really want to know the future. I hoped Esmerelda couldn't see anything unusual in her crystal ball or the palm of my hand. Just a normal life. That's all I really wanted.

It was dark inside, and except for one candle floating in a dish of water on top of a small table, the room seemed deserted and smelled strongly of burning sweetgrass.

"Sit down," a voice called out of the darkness. I jumped. A petite woman stepped out from behind a partition in the wall. She gestured to a chair and I sat. She took the chair opposite. In the light of the candle I could see she was very slight with long black hair and olive skin. She wore a thick band of silver bracelets on her forearm. She smiled and looked directly at me.

"Give me your hand." I hesitated for a moment, then placed my left hand on the table. She picked it up and held it firmly in her own. She closed her eyes. I hoped with all my might that I wouldn't feel anything or see anything and neither would she.

She spread my palm open and ran the tip of her finger down the longest line in my skin there. I felt the warmth of her hand under mine. "You want me to tell you that what you're doing is the right thing. Keeping this *secret* to yourself." I felt a shiver race up my arms. *How can she know that?* I wondered. She let my hand rest on the table.

"I can't do that." Her eyes held my gaze. "Only you know how difficult it is to keep something as big as this to yourself, eh?"

Her hand disappeared beneath the table and emerged again with a long, brown cigarette in a holder. It looked almost like a cigar. She lit it and inhaled slowly, then blew three perfect rings of smoke into the air over my head. I watched them float by until they faded into the blackness.

"I wanted to have a quiet life too. A life like everyone else. But some things just never go away. They keep calling." She took another long drag of her cigarette and let the smoke out slowly.

She lifted a velvet cloth off the table, revealing a slim stack of cards. "Let's see what the cards have to say." She picked them up and shuffled them gently. They were worn from use. She laid out twelve cards in a fan and then looked up at me.

"Pick one. Don't think about it. Just pick the first you see." I reached out and picked a card near the middle of the fan and pushed it toward her.

She flipped it, revealing the picture of a woman in a white toga carrying a torch in one hand.

"Ah! The Light Bearer." She turned the card so I could see it. "She goes into dark places—places no one else wants to go—and brings back all the gifts of the world." She held the card up to her forehead and closed her eyes. "The Light Bearer comes to tell you"—she paused and smiled—"Harmony . . . that to whom much is given, much is expected." My stomach tightened as she spoke. "Events have been set into motion," she said matter-of-factly, and shuffled the card back into the fan, and the fan into the deck. She covered the deck once again with the cloth, then sat back and closed her eyes.

She held her hand out to me and I gave her mine. She laughed. "No, my dear. That's all. That'll be three tickets."

"Oh," I said, blushing. "Of course, here you are." I laid the crumpled orange tickets on the table and pushed them in her direction.

She slipped them into her pocket, dropped her cigarette on the dirt floor and ground it out with the ball of her foot. "The weather is changing," she said, pressing her index finger to her right temple. "You better go find your friends." She disappeared then, behind the partition, and the room became quiet. I sat there for a moment, feeling a little dizzy. Feeling like something had changed, though I didn't know what. I took a deep breath, stood up and walked to the front of the tent, pulled back the flap and stumbled out into the light.

"So how was it?" Shawnie was waiting eagerly at the entrance as I came out. "Did she tell you your future? Did she talk about your psychic powers, your telekinetic abilities? Did she give you—"

"I guess so."

"You guess so? Well, what did she say?" Shawnie asked impatiently.

"That the weather's changing." Shawnie looked puzzled and glanced up at the sky.

"Not a cloud. Not one single cloud." She looked disappointed. "Is that all?"

I shrugged. "I didn't really understand all she said."

"Well, come on, let's go. Caleb's waiting for us at the concession stand. The line is a mile long. I'm trying to convince him to go see the Magnificent Mutant Man with me. What do you think? Want to go? It's a once-in-a-lifetime opportunity." I looked at her blankly. My mind was still back in the fortune-teller's tent.

"Don't worry, Harmony. It was only three tickets. What do fortune-tellers know, anyway? It doesn't matter."

It does matter, I thought as I let her guide me forward. *It matters a lot.*

★   ★   ★

Shawnie tried to drag us into the Magnificent Mutant Man's tent, assuring us that we'd never have the chance to see the bizarre effects of neurofibromatosis ever again, but I refused. I wanted to move on to the midway and put some distance between myself and the sideshow alley.

As we walked along together, Esmerelda's words swam around in my mind like crazy fish. What did she mean "events have been set in motion"? Was that something she said to everyone as they left her tent, just to keep them on edge? Just to make it seem like she knew what she was talking about? Maybe. But then how did she know my name, my secret? Something about her words seemed true.

★   ★   ★

We had time for one more thing before Shawnie and Caleb had to leave, so Caleb asked me to ride the Ferris wheel with him. My heart started off on its racetrack again, and Shawnie patted Caleb on the back. "Way to go, cuz," she said, and winked at me. "Meet me in front of the grandstand when you're through."

"Harmony, honey," she said, turning to hug me. "I'll see you at school on Monday. And think about coming to the reunion with us, okay?"

"Okay," I said, hugging her back. Shawnie and Caleb had invited me to the Pawlett Family Reunion the last weekend in June. It was going to be at Shawnie's house. Caleb assured me that the whole thing would take place outside under big tents, so I wouldn't have to worry about microwaves or smoke alarms. I said I'd love to go.

There was only a short line for the Ferris wheel. It was tall, and each seat was a different color. We were given a red one, buckled in by a man with a tattoo on his left arm and sent up into the sky.

I'd never been on anything so high in my life. It wasn't like the Centipede, where you felt the motion but were going so fast you couldn't see more than a blur. The Ferris wheel was open and going so slowly, I could see everything. I could see all the way to the mountains. I thought about Wilson and Anthony and McAllister up there where night comes so much earlier because of all the trees blocking out the sun, and I felt truly fortunate to be out in the world, far away from tending to Willa and our plans to save the Old People.

The light was beginning to fade. It was the time of day when the sky is pink and everything turns soft and dreamy, as if you're looking through colored glasses.

"That's where my house is," I said to Caleb, pointing toward the mountains. "Up at the top of that tallest one."

"Don't you get nosebleeds living that high up?" he said, grinning.

"No, I'm used to it. Of course you'd probably get one, living in the flatland of Delaware County like you do."

"You gonna spend your whole life way up there?" Caleb asked. I shook my head.

"I'm going to travel the world with my uncle Felix one day." I looked over at Caleb to see what his reaction was to that idea. I thought for a minute that he might laugh, but his mountain face got all serious.

"I believe you will, Harmony McClean" was all he said.

We were silent for a time and in that silence, it occurred to me that I hadn't known Caleb very long, but already he knew something about me that it took most people a long time to figure out: that I always meant what I said. I studied Caleb as we sat there going around and around, and I made a permanent picture in my mind of his face and his hands, so close to my own on the seat. I made a picture of the lights of Carson City and the tents below us and the evening sky.

"I like your name," Caleb said, staring out at the mountains. "It suits you."

"Felix named me. He's a big believer in the aesthetic arrangement of things—numbers, planets, music. Harmony is one of his greatest passions, so he named me after it."

"It fits," Caleb said. "There is something aesthetically arranged about you." He laughed, then stopped and looked me straight in the eyes. "No, really, there *is* something . . . about you."

"Maybe I'm just the only person you know who can set microwaves on fire with their mind," I said, trying to say it before he did. Caleb laughed.

"Maybe. But that's explainable. You're just telekinetic or something. That's what Shawnie says. It's not that," he continued. "It's . . . the way you are. You have a lot of light inside you. It makes people want to be near you."

"Really?" I asked. I thought most people on the mountain went out of their way to avoid any direct contact with me.

I wondered if *he* wanted to be near me, but I didn't ask.

"Harmony McClean, after you save your trees and

before you travel the world, will you come visit me?" he asked, looking out at the sky.

I didn't even think before I spoke. "Yes, Caleb, I will."

Gradually the wheel slowed. It took a long time for all the people to get off and since we were the first on, it looked like we'd be the last off. But I didn't want to get off at all. I wanted to stay up until it got dark and the stars started to come out. Then I could show Caleb what Arcturus looked like, and Vega and the Corona Borealis.

I guess that's what made it happen—my strong desire. The Ferris wheel stopped with Caleb and me close to the top, and it took a full hour to get it going again. In that time, Venus showed herself bright in the east, the North Star blinked above us and Caleb bent down and gently kissed me. It was so light, his kiss. Like a feather brushing over my lips. So gentle, I wasn't sure it had happened at all. I opened my eyes. He smiled, put his head back and gazed up at the sky and I knew what he was doing. He was making one last wish before we came back to earth.

★   ★   ★

Felix and Nettie Mae were eating by the time I arrived at the picnic grounds. They pretended not to have been worried about me, but I could tell by the way Nettie Mae's faced relaxed when she saw me that they had been.

"Harmony, we're sure glad to see you," Felix said,

wrapping me up in one of Nettie Mae's sweaters. "Thought you might have flown off one of those fast rides and spun all the way back up to the stars."

"Well," I said, my face all flushed. "It was kind of like that."

Nettie Mae gave me a curious look, pulled a turkey sandwich and a bottle of juice out of the picnic basket and offered them to me. I wasn't very hungry. My stomach felt all jumpy and nervous, but I took the juice to be polite.

Sitting there in the cool grass, bundled up in Nettie Mae's soft sweater, I reached up and ran my fingers along my lips, remembering what it felt like to have someone else's touching them.

It seemed like this wonderful day could not end. I think Felix and Nettie Mae felt it too as we all huddled together looking up at the sky.

"You know," Felix said, putting an arm around each of us. "I do believe the planets are singing tonight."

★

CHAPTER
ELEVEN

★

I DIDN'T GET the feeling until we were on our way back up the mountain, but when it came upon me, it was powerful—like a bolt of lightning striking right inside the front seat of the truck.

"What is it, Harmony?" Felix asked as I flinched beside him. He was trying to keep his eyes on the road as fat drops of rain began falling on the windshield. The weather had changed, just like Esmerelda had said it would.

"Nothing. Just a feeling."

"What kind of feeling?" Nettie Mae poked her head between Felix and me from the backseat. I wasn't sure if

I should say, though I knew what it was. The image of Willa's face flashed through my mind as a wave of heat came over me. My whole left arm seized up in pain, and I doubled over. Felix pulled the truck off to the side of the road, and Nettie Mae got out and came around to the front.

"Harmony, honey. What is it? Are you sick?" She held her wrist to my forehead. I shook my head.

"It isn't me," I said, afraid of the words even as they came out of my mouth.

"What do you mean?" Felix asked. The pain subsided for a moment and I looked up into his face and then into Nettie Mae's, and I knew I couldn't hold it back from them any longer. But I wanted to. More than anything in the world, I wanted to. I knew that as soon as I told them what I was feeling, nothing would ever be the same.

The rain hit the windshield hard and thunder cracked in the distance.

I sat wedged between Felix and Nettie Mae—the two people who loved me most in the world—and I felt a terrible loneliness come over me. I had an urgent longing to stop everything at that moment. I wanted the storm to last all night and keep us trapped on the mountainside with our memories fresh from the fair— the feeling of Caleb, the spin of the rides. I didn't want to go forward. I didn't want this perfect day to end with Willa. I didn't want her to have the last word on our happiness, but I knew she would.

"It's Willa," I said finally. "Sometimes I can . . . feel things," I explained. "Feel what other people feel."

"Willa's bad off, isn't she," Nettie Mae said as if she already knew.

I nodded. "She's waiting for you, Nettie Mae. She's got to ask you something before she goes." Just then, another pain swept over me and I buried my head in Nettie Mae's shoulder. She held me tight and touched Felix on the arm and I knew she was giving him a look.

"I'll do my best, darlin'," Felix said, putting the truck into second gear to climb a rough stretch of road near Hamlin's Gorge. "But I'm not going to put us in danger."

For the next hour, we all sat in the front seat watching Felix navigate the muddy, rocky road up to the house. In spring, when the rains come on heavy, they'll wash out a bridge and sweep the road away entirely—until there's nothing but a big mud hole where once there was a road.

As Felix drove on, the raindrops became a downpour and no matter how fast the windshield wipers went, they weren't fast enough. Felix had to pull off several times and wait for the rain to let up before we could move on.

The pain in my arm subsided, but left a heavy feeling in my stomach. I'd thought when the time finally came for me to tell them the truth, I would feel relieved, but I didn't. I felt like a baby starling before its wings grew in, vulnerable and scared about what was to come. Nettie Mae and Felix must've had a thousand questions for me, but no one said a word.

We finally pulled into the driveway at eleven o'clock. Wilson leapt off the front porch and came bounding toward us, wagging his tail and baying in his mournful way. The chickens were all aflutter running around the yard, which was a mess. One of the big oak trees on the Tennessee side lay smack in the center of Felix's studio—a great hole had been ripped in the roof and the chicken coop was smashed to pieces. A few chickens lay on the ground, unconscious or dead. I couldn't tell which.

Felix and I slowly slid out of the truck and stood staring at the tree.

"Lord have mercy" was all Felix said as he walked over to the hole in the roof to survey the damage.

"I'll get the chickens, Nettie Mae," I yelled to her as she headed into the house. She didn't hear me. She had only one thing on her mind: getting her bundle and reaching Willa in time.

As I gathered the remaining chickens, Nettie Mae emerged from the house and unhitched Anthony from the maple tree. She had that single-minded look in her eyes. This was to be a solo trip. Nettie Mae always went alone to births and deaths. It was her custom. She didn't want Felix or me with her. It used to bother me that she wouldn't take me to births, and I'd told her so. She said she might take me when I could be of help, but for now she liked to have the house as quiet as possible. She didn't want a lot of folks milling around when souls were busy coming or going.

Nettie Mae climbed onto Anthony, and Felix ran up beside her. I couldn't hear what they were saying over the squawking of the chickens. I saw Felix shake his head and then walk over to the porch.

"Stubborn woman," I heard Felix say as he threw his hat down on the steps. "Never, in all my life, have I met a woman as stubborn."

Nettie Mae started up the trail, then turned around as if reconsidering and motioned me toward her. My heart sank.

"Harmony, if you're feeling up to it, I'd appreciate you coming along. In case I need you. In case Willa needs you."

I didn't say anything. I just took the extra slicker and boots she handed me, put them on and followed her into the fog.

★   ★   ★

It was one of those stormy nights that made me wonder about spirits in the woods. Every tree groaned and in between showers of rain an eerie silence hung in the air, accompanied every so often by the drip of water off leaves.

It took us close to an hour to negotiate our way to Willa's house. The trail was one big puddle of mud, and every once in a while Anthony stepped wrong and we had to pull him free. Eventually Willa's house came into view. We could see it from the cairn—the only light in a vast sea of trees and darkness.

When we reached the front porch, Nettie Mae and I exchanged looks. Everything was too still. She slid off Anthony's back, and with an urgency I'd never seen in her before, she leapt up the front steps and was through the door and into the house ahead of me. I tied up Anthony and followed her.

Once inside Willa's kitchen, I pulled the slicker over my head and peeled off Nettie Mae's damp sweater. It still smelled like the fair—popcorn and fried peppers. There were no embers left in Willa's woodstove. The house was miserable and damp. I wished I were home with Felix.

On rainy nights, I like plenty of light. I usually keep the lamp in my room burning until dawn even though Felix says that's asking for a house fire, but it warms something inside me to have light around. And food. I'm like Nettie Mae in that way. When there's a crisis, I feel a strong need to feed people and light lamps and generally make things as normal as possible even when it seems that things may never be normal again.

I walked to the bedroom and stood in the doorway. Nettie Mae was bent over Willa, her index finger checking for a pulse.

"Willa," she whispered. "Can you hear me?" A slight wheezing sound came from Willa's chest. Nettie Mae motioned me to her side, but I couldn't move. I knew that if I walked over to Willa, I'd have to touch her. I'd have to feel what she was feeling. My feet felt as though they had grown right down into the floorboards and would never move again. I could only hear my breath, as if magnified by a stethoscope, and my heart beating in my ears. My mind went blank and all I could think about was my boots and how they were making big brown puddles on Willa's clean floor. "My boots are making a mess and Willa won't be pleased."

"Harmony?" Nettie Mae sounded concerned. "What's wrong?"

How could I tell Nettie Mae what it felt like to touch Willa and be swept into her world, hold her hand and hear the workings of her mind? Nettie Mae waited. Willa waited.

I knew Willa wouldn't let go until she'd told Nettie Mae what she had to tell her, but she was beyond speech. I was the only one who could help her now.

My legs started up on their own, walking me forward to kneel me down beside the bed. I gathered every ounce of courage in my body and took hold of her hand. I expected Willa's wrathful voice in my ears, her screeching, but that's not what I heard. Her voice was like a birdsong. It was a whisper.

I looked at Willa's hard, bony face and all I could feel was a slight tugging tenderness in my heart for her. I'd never felt that before. And then the words came like they did with Mr. Carver, but softly, timidly. I told them to Nettie Mae as my throat tightened.

"Did I sing like a bird, Nettie? Did they like it? Did they all like it?"

Tears came to Nettie Mae's eyes and she bent close to Willa. She put her hand over mine, over Willa's.

"You had a voice like an angel, Willa Henshaw," she whispered in her ear. "You always did."

A sound came out of Willa like steam released from a kettle. Her whole chest relaxed and her face, too. Nettie Mae put her fingers on Willa's wrist and looked up at me. Willa was gone. Or maybe not really gone. I could feel her in the room and still hear her singing in my head. Nettie Mae stood up, walked over to the window, pushed the curtains aside and opened it wide so Willa's spirit could depart. She reached for her bundle, pulled out some sage to burn and began singing her turtle song.

I knelt there looking down at Willa Henshaw, the woman who had once caused me such grief and had taken so much energy from Nettie Mae. And I couldn't feel anything bad toward her anymore. I thought, *She's free now*. And I wished her peace.

★

CHAPTER TWELVE

★

NETTIE MAE'S FEVER started the next day. The doctor from Hildeen said it was exhaustion. A direct result of Nettie Mae's weakened heart, being out in the cold rain and the effort of bringing Willa's body down the mountain.

I blamed myself. If I hadn't felt Willa calling, Nettie Mae never would have gone out in the storm and up the mountain in the first place. I might have helped Willa, but I'd made things worse for Nettie Mae. Felix disagreed. He said I did everything right. "Nettie would have gone up that mountain with or without you telling her. Besides who could ever *tell* Nettie Mae anything?" he reminded me. But I didn't believe him.

A deep silence fell over our house. The cavelike walls no longer resonated the notes of Nettie Mae's off-key Cherokee songs or the sweet melodies of Felix's fiddle. The studio was just as silent. No pings. No hammering. No Felix tinkering with gadgets. Just a gaping hole in the roof that the chickens had taken to nesting in, in place of the coop. The few remaining hens pecked around in the dirt searching for feed that we'd forgotten to throw out, looking dazed and bewildered, trying to find something recognizable from their old lives before the storm. At night they looked for safety from foxes inside the damp remains of Felix's Harmony Box.

That's exactly how I felt—adrift in the sudden silence. I couldn't shake the feeling that it was all my fault. If I'd only kept it to myself a little longer, Nettie Mae would be well. But she wasn't well. She could barely lift her head from the pillow without getting winded. I wanted to help Nettie Mae, but I didn't know how. Nothing happened when I touched her hand. I tried focusing my thoughts on her, hoping that like the fire in the woodstove, I could ignite that spark inside her again. But it didn't work. Nothing worked.

I felt like I'd dropped off into another universe where there wasn't anything familiar to grab on to and where anything could happen. Like the black holes in space Felix has told me about, places where gravity is so strong that not even light can escape. Nothing can break away from the fierce grip of a black hole.

Even whole stars can get sucked into them and disappear forever.

★   ★   ★

Nettie Mae had been bedridden for a week when Shawnie came to visit.

"Harmony McClean, are you there?" There was a loud rap on the kitchen door. It was eight o'clock on a Saturday morning. The house had been so quiet all week that the knock startled me awake. I jumped out of bed and ran for the door.

"Hey, Shawnie," I whispered, opening the latch. "Come on in. Quiet, Nettie Mae is sleeping."

"Nettie Mae is sleeping at this hour? I thought she got up with the chickens."

"She used to," I said, closing the door.

"Where have you been, Harmony? I was expecting to see you at school. I've been worried."

"I've been right here, taking care of Nettie Mae. She's sick. Real sick. She's been in bed for a week." Shawnie's eyes lit up.

"What's she got, Harmony? The flu? The grippe? There's a nasty stomach virus going around. . . ."

"No. It isn't sick like that," I said, rubbing the sleep out of my eyes. "It's more serious. Doc Edwards says she's exhausted, but I think that's just a gentle way of telling us her heart is all worn out." Shawnie and I exchanged looks. "There's no cure for that."

"Oh, Harmony, honey. Isn't there anything anybody can do?" I shook my head.

"What about you? Can you help her by using your powers?"

"I've tried. Nothing works. Besides, my *powers* are what put Nettie Mae into that bed in the first place. I don't want to do any more damage."

"What do you mean?" Shawnie asked. I told her the whole story. When I was finished, she sat down in the kitchen chair and looked at me curiously.

"So, you got Nettie Mae to Willa in time and you helped Willa die, and now just because Nettie Mae's sick it's all your fault?"

I nodded. "I've been hoping that these powers will go away so I can't hurt anyone else. It was all a mistake anyway," I said, throwing a log into the woodstove.

"What was a mistake?"

"Me. Having this gift to begin with. I've never known what to do with it. The minute I start enjoying it, having fun with it, it changes. It gets complicated and serious. It affects other people. I love the feeling of it. I love knowing I can think about something and it might happen. I wish it were simple, but it never is. Maybe I can give it back, or maybe if I just ignore it, it'll start to fade away on its own. That could happen, couldn't it?"

Shawnie stood up and walked over to the window, took a deep breath and turned around to face me. "I can't believe you, Harmony. I really can't. Do you know how many people wish they could do what you can do? Do you have any idea how amazing it could be if you didn't keep it all locked away? Sometimes I think all you care about is yourself. Keeping everything nice and simple for *you*. *'I just want to eat cotton candy,'* " Shawnie said, mimicking me at the fair. " *'And ride the Centipede and make believe I'm like everybody else.'* Well, you're not like everybody else. You have a gift, and that gift isn't simple." I shrugged. "Maybe you're right, Harmony. Maybe you don't deserve to have such a gift if all it'll ever be is some bag of tricks you can pull out every once in a while at a party to entertain people." Shawnie's voice had risen from a whisper to a restrained yell. I could hear Felix moving around in the next room.

I put my finger to my lips. "It's not as simple as you think, Shawnie," I whispered. "You don't know. You don't live with it every day. There are consequences to being who I am."

"There are always consequences," Shawnie said. "You think Mother Teresa didn't have consequences? Or Gandhi, or Martin Luther King? But they didn't hide themselves away on a mountaintop or in a cave because they were afraid to be who they were.

"Maybe you can't save Nettie Mae's life, but you've helped her—you're still helping her. And if she decides to stay or go, it has nothing to do with you. You're not God, Harmony. You just have to do your best, use your gift, but you can't control the outcome . . . of anything." She stopped and took a deep breath.

"You're my best friend, Harmony, but sometimes

you make me mad. There are people out there who could help you understand this, if you'd let them. And people you could help, if you just get out of your own way."

The bedroom door creaked open and Felix emerged, dressed for the day. Or maybe he'd slept in his clothes. It was hard to tell.

"Mornin', Shawnie," he said with a tired smile. "What brings you up here at this hour of the day?"

"Oh, hi, Mr. McGillicuddy. I'm just checking on Harmony. I didn't mean to disturb you so early. I'm sorry to hear about your troubles."

"Well, thank you. I think Nettie's feeling a tad better this morning. You going to stay for some breakfast?"

"No, thank you. I already ate," Shawnie said. "I really need to be getting home, but I'll stop by later in the week to check on you both."

"Why, that's mighty nice," Felix said, putting a kettle on top of the woodstove and taking a carton of eggs out of the icebox. I walked Shawnie out into the yard.

"Harmony, I'm just telling you how I feel. You can be mad at me if you want to. But I just can't stand by and watch you throw all this away without saying anything."

"I'm not mad, Shawnie. I just don't know anything anymore. Nettie Mae has never been sick. I feel like there's nothing I can do and it's all my fault."

Shawnie reached over and hugged me. "I'm sorry if my words were hard, but I don't think your powers are to blame here. If you could learn more about them, they might just be able to help you."

"Thanks, Shawnie." I hugged her and she gave me a few more words of advice, then headed back down the mountain.

After Shawnie left, I spent the rest of the day cooking and keeping the woodstove full. I thought about what she'd said, but I still couldn't let go of the fact that I'd ruined it for all of us. One moment we were happy and content, and the next our lives were turned upside down.

It seemed like a lifetime ago, instead of one week, that Felix and Nettie Mae were riding the merry-go-round at the fair and I was sitting at the top of the Ferris wheel with Caleb, his arm around me. Whenever I thought about it, I felt a longing inside that was so strong, it frightened me. Up on this mountain, the rest of the world seemed so far away that I couldn't touch it. And Caleb was out there—in the world I couldn't reach.

All I could think to do was pray—to the spirits of the forest and Nettie Mae's ancestors and the stars. I prayed for Nettie Mae and Felix and myself. I prayed that the three of us would be together again like we used to be—circling around each other like the planets, making music. I prayed and I waited.

And then something happened on the last day of April that none of us expected. After six straight days of rain, the sun came out. The sky cleared to the blue of a chicory flower, and the Spring Beauties outside Nettie Mae's window bloomed for the first time—sending a fragrance like honey into her room. And there was a sound, too; faint but rumbling. The sound of trucks far off in the distance making their way up the mountain.

★

CHAPTER
THIRTEEN

★

It was almost a relief to hear the sound of engines approaching our house on that sunny morning. A deep rumble like thunder, like new life, winding its way to us.

Felix pulled out the letter from Burston Jones that had arrived in yesterday's mail. He read and reread it. Nothing mentioned a change in schedule. It stated most clearly that cutting would not begin until May twentieth, after the spring rains. But nonetheless, the trucks came.

"Well, if this isn't the worst possible time for them to come, I don't know what is, Harmony. We haven't even begun building the platforms and even if we had,

there isn't enough time to gather anyone to help us."
Felix and I sat together at the breakfast table looking
out at the first sunny day since the Huntsville Fair. We
were trying to prepare ourselves for what this beautiful
day might bring, still reeling from what the previous
days had brought us.

"We're like two soldiers weary from battle," I told
Felix. "Hearing the enemy approaching and not having
the slightest idea how to defend ourselves."

"No such thing as an enemy," Felix reminded me.
"No enemy inside you. No enemy outside you. No enemy." Felix's favorite motto. I nodded. "Can't think of
them as our enemy, Harmony. But you're right about
one thing—there's going to be a lot of man power out
there pretty soon, and our energy is mighty low." Felix
gazed out the window. I'd never seen him look so tired.
Burying Willa and worrying about Nettie Mae had
taken a lot out of him.

I wanted Felix to say, "We can turn any situation
around in our favor, Harmony," but he was silent as we
both stood up and walked into Nettie Mae's room.

She was propped up on pillows, her face pale as she
stared out through the thin white curtains of her window.

"What's that rumbling I hear, Felix?" Nettie Mae
asked in a weak voice. "Surely with that sun, it can't be
more thunder."

I looked over at Felix, wondering what he was going
to tell her.

"Not thunder, darlin'. Trucks."

"Can't be trucks," Nettie Mae said, alarmed and bringing herself up on her elbows.

"Now, Nettie, you're not to get yourself worked up about this. They've come early. That's all. Harmony and I have a backup plan. Don't we, Harmony?"

I nodded, thinking that was the first time I had ever heard Felix tell an outright lie to Nettie Mae.

"Now, how are you and a bit of a girl like Harmony going to hold off a bunch of loggers?" Nettie Mae asked him.

"We have it all worked out, Nettie." Felix didn't sound too convincing, and I could tell by the look on Nettie Mae's face that she believed we were licked before we started. If she thought we were going to lose the Old People, then she might just give up herself.

I sat there staring at the two of them, and an idea began to rise in me. Maybe I could still make it all right again. If I could save the trees, maybe Nettie Mae would get better. Maybe I could use my gift one more time before I gave it back.

"I have to go, Nettie Mae. I have a lot of work to do before they get here." I stood up and headed for the door, and Felix followed me into the kitchen.

"What do you have on your mind, Harmony?" he asked, leaning his shoulder against the door frame. "You getting a feeling again?" We'd both been so busy since the night of the storm that Felix hadn't asked me any questions about what had happened at Willa's. I knew he was bursting with curiosity. I sat down at the kitchen table.

"Sometimes I get feelings, Felix, and sometimes I don't. Sometimes I can just think about things and . . . they happen." He nodded, not taking his eyes off me.

"Maybe you better sit down, and I'll show you what I mean." I gestured to the chair opposite me and he lowered himself into it. I felt like I was back in Esmerelda's tent.

I pulled two spoons from the basket on the table and placed them in front of me, held my hand over them and waited. I'd never done it for an audience before. I wasn't even sure if I could. I closed my eyes and tried to feel the spoons. I thought of them twirling around a bit and after a minute, that's exactly what they did. Felix jumped in his seat with his eyes wide. Then he laughed a little, nervously. When the spoons stopped, I looked up at him. He was staring at me, his mouth open.

"Can you do it again?" he asked, as excited as a little boy.

I nodded my head and they twirled again.

"I have never seen anything like that in all my life. I've read about it, though. Telekinesis, isn't that it?" I smiled. I should have known Felix would know the name for it.

"My God, Harmony. How long have you been able to do this?" He didn't wait for my answer. "Can you do it with other things?"

I nodded again. "I can. I can light fires and move crystals. I'm not exactly sure of all I can do yet, Felix. I haven't known about it that long. To tell you the truth, I've been a little afraid to find out. I've been keeping it to myself."

"That's a mighty big thing to keep to yourself, honey. How come you didn't tell us?"

I shrugged my shoulders. "I didn't want to burden you."

Felix smiled. "Wouldn't have been a burden. Would have been a delight. Maybe that's what you were worried about, eh? Me asking you all kinds of questions?" I nodded. Felix stood up. He walked over to my chair and patted my head with his hand, like he always does. "I am very proud of you, Harmony, and I thank you for gathering the courage to tell me this." I felt relief settle inside me.

"Now," said Felix. "What's this plan you got cooking in your mind?"

★   ★   ★

For the next three weeks, as the buds opened into shiny new leaves on the oak trees and the robins came back to the mountains—and the logging trucks rolled into our yard—I greeted the men from the Great Northern Lumber Company with a cheerful smile and a pot of hot coffee. I thanked them for helping us with the trees. And every evening, when the men went back to their tents to sleep, I'd sit up inside their skidders and log loaders and think about axles breaking.

In the mornings, when the men arrived fresh for a

day's work, they found that their machines' engines wouldn't turn over. I sympathized with their dilemma and offered them more coffee as they spent the rest of the day repairing the damage I'd done.

Felix helped in his own way. He told them stories of how things like this happen in the mountains all the time, and that folks who live here blame it on spirits. Felix said only a fool would believe in spirits, though, when there was a perfectly sound scientific explanation for the whole thing. Then he'd launch into a complex theory of energy lines and vortexes. He told them it was a proven fact that there were currents running under the ground, and where those currents cross each other, the energy is so concentrated that it is impossible to operate machinery or electrical devices without things going haywire. It sounded like he was talking about me.

Felix gave them a tour of his studio, which had begun to take shape again, though the Harmony Box still lay in pieces. He offered them his theories on free energy, life on other planets and his latest obsession, telekinesis. I could tell he was having a fine time sharing his wealth of knowledge and even though it seemed an unlikely audience, they were so restless waiting for new parts to come up the mountain that I think some of them actually listened. In a strange way, I was glad to have them here. They were a distraction to us from the turn our lives had taken. And Felix was coming back to his vibrant, hopeful self.

The lumbermen did all seem to agree on one thing, and that was that no human being was messing with their equipment. It was clear that Nettie Mae was too sick to get out of bed, I was only a young girl and Felix was too friendly to be under suspicion. He always offered to help them repair their chain saws and often invited them in for lunch.

The lumbermen started spending most of their time in our kitchen eating omelettes and bemoaning the fact that they couldn't get their work done and had families to get back home to.

Some days I spent the whole morning and part of the afternoon cooking and cleaning up after them. There were six lumberjacks altogether and the more time I spent talking to them the more I found myself liking these men. Felix was right. They weren't our enemies; they were just trying to make a living and feed their families. Somehow, though, I still wished they could see what they were doing. If they cut down the Old People, they'd be disrupting a whole way of life for the forest, for us, and for the spirits of the Cherokee, who still lingered everywhere. I thought if one of them could sit up in Nula and feel the sap running through her trunk and hear her branches whispering in the wind, they'd change their minds about what they were doing. They'd understand how every single leaf of a tree has its place.

As the three days allotted for the cutting turned into three weeks, I had to be more careful about my nighttime activites, but I didn't mind. If it helped Nettie Mae get better, I'd do anything. I'd pull myself up to the top of Nula after the men had gone back to camp for the night. I could stay up there until right before dawn, watching everything from high up in Nula's branches and doing what I needed to do.

I was so preoccupied with saving the Old People and making sure the lumbermen didn't suspect anything that I didn't spend as much time as I wanted to with Nettie Mae. One evening she called me into her room and asked me to sit on the bed. She looked a little better. She had some color in her cheeks. It seemed that every day we kept the saws from cutting into the Old People, she was gaining strength.

"Harmony, I want you to know how proud I am of what you did for Willa and what you're doing to save the Old People. You're quite a mystery to me." I looked down at my hands. "Quite a lovely mystery." I lifted my head.

"You have a powerful gift. Don't be afraid of it. Use it well." I nodded. "I'd die a happy woman knowing the Old People are safe," Nettie Mae said, and looked at me.

I felt my stomach drop. "We're going to save the trees, Nettie Mae. We are. And after the loggers leave, you and Felix and I will make an offering to them on the solstice, like we always do."

"You seem pretty sure about that." I nodded. Nettie Mae smiled. "Let's just take it a moment at a time." Her eyes were tired, but there was a strange spark behind them as if she held a secret deep inside herself. She lifted the blanket beside her and pulled out her bundle. She pushed it in my direction. "If you could hold on to this for me, Harmony, I'd sure appreciate it. Doc Edwards will come up once a month to check on folks, but he won't be needing this. I'd like you to have it. Keep it in the family."

I nodded, knowing what this meant and not wanting to believe she was giving it to me. I didn't want to take it, but Nettie Mae was waiting and so I reached out and picked up the bundle. She lay back on the pillows and closed her eyes.

"You go out into the fresh air. I'll rest a little now." She patted my hand. I could think of nothing to say to her. I slipped quietly out the door and ran up to the rise, where I always sat with Felix. I carried the bundle under my arm and when I reached the highest spot, I placed it on the ground in front of me. I lay down and put my face in the soft grass and let my tears soak into the ground. When there were no tears left, I rolled onto my back and looked up at the sky.

I searched out all the stars I knew of and some I didn't. I thought of the stories Nettie Mae had woven for me around those pinpricks of light. I remembered the night we lay on the roof of the house staring up at the heavens and Nettie Mae told me that to pray on any star was to have a prayer answered.

I found Arcturus, and keeping it in view, I got down on my knees and prayed. Though maybe it was more of a bargain than a prayer and maybe not a fair one at that, given I no longer wanted what I was offering.

"I'm giving it back!" I yelled up at the constellation. "You can have it." The tears began again, streaming down my face. "You take it and leave Nettie Mae, okay?" The stars glared coldly down at me. I stayed on my knees waiting for an answer. I hoped with all my might that someone out there had heard me. Maybe Cygnus, the swan star, was awake, and would fly along the stream of the Milky Way and down to Earth and take this burden—this terrible feeling deep in my belly that no matter what I did, Nettie Mae was leaving us behind.

★

CHAPTER
FOURTEEN

★

NETTIE MAE DIED on the solstice, the first day of summer. Three days after the lumbermen pulled out of our driveway with all their equipment and headed down the mountain after almost two months of unsuccessful logging.

The night before, Nettie Mae had asked us to open the window for her before we went to bed. Felix pulled the curtains aside, undid the latch and pushed the windows out toward the night. But we didn't go to bed. Felix and I stayed up with her. Waiting. She could barely lift her head off the pillow. We knew she was fading fast. We took turns reading her favorite poems, and Felix played his fiddle as soft as a whisper. I held Nettie Mae's hand and Felix hummed a tune. Around midnight, he told me to get some fresh air. I didn't want to leave, though I couldn't bear to stay and say good-bye either. I knew there were things Felix needed to say to Nettie Mae without me there. I crept quietly downstairs and outside as I had done for the past month, and pulled myself up to the top of Nula and cried myself to sleep in her arms.

High up in those soft branches, I had a dream. I was sitting on the rise with Felix and Nettie Mae. We were looking up at Venus, bright in the eastern sky, and Felix had his Harmony Box on the ground in front of him, only it was big, almost as big as a house. He had to climb up on a ladder just to tune the dials.

"Don't bother with that now, Felix," Nettie Mae scolded in her practical voice, gesturing him to her side. "Hurry or you'll miss the best part." Just then a comet streaked across the blackness and burst into flames. "That's it," she said, pointing up at the fireball and sitting back with a sigh. "That's the way I want to go."

I woke in the early morning. The first light of dawn filtered through Nula's branches and danced about on my face. As I woke, there was a brief moment of peace in my mind, when I felt that all things were as they should be, and I had nothing ahead of me but a day of baking bread and studying the astronomical theories of Copernicus. Then I remembered Nettie Mae, and I sat up with a start. I shinnied my way down to the ground and walked quietly back into the house. Felix was sitting in his rocking chair in the living room. He looked like a little boy in his flannel pajamas—his face newly washed and soft in the morning light. He motioned me to him and I curled up in his lap. I nestled myself down into his warmth and together we sat in the silence, watching the morning sun flood the forest with light.

I turned my head up and looked into Felix's face.

He nodded his head. "She's gone, darlin'."

★   ★   ★

We buried Nettie Mae at the foot of Nula. It was a windy day, warm and full of sun. The kind of day you wish for all winter long. Felix and I dressed Nettie Mae in her favorite blue linen dress that she usually reserved for weddings, and gently placed her in a pine box that Felix had made.

I wore my Sunday church dress that I never wore, as we never went to church, and Felix wore his one good suit and tie and the felt hat with the turkey feather in it—the one Nettie Mae said made him look almost Cherokee.

Felix picked a bouquet of wildflowers, a bouquet so big and unruly that we couldn't even tie a ribbon around it. They lay all spread out on the loose earth over Nettie Mae like a colorful Chinese fan. I placed a loaf of freshly baked bread next to them because Nettie Mae said it's often a long journey to the other side, and even spirits get hungry. Sila, Jonathan, Greta and McAllister came down. And Shawnie came up from the Hollow. She didn't say anything; for once, she had no advice to give. She simply wrapped me in her arms and didn't let go until we were both soaking wet with tears.

Then we all stood in the silence and listened to the wind, which we figured was more to Nettie Mae's liking than a whole slew of formal words. Felix took out his fiddle and played "In the Cool of the Evening" sweet and low. Wilson, hiding behind the raspberry bushes, whined along with the melody the whole time.

I stood there looking up at Nula still standing tall, watching over Nettie Mae, and even though my own heart was heavy with grief, I knew the spirits of the land were pleased with what we had done to save the trees and would lead Nettie Mae safely to the land of her ancestors.

★ ★ ★

In the following days everything moved in slow motion, and I wondered if the hole Nettie Mae had left behind would ever be filled. Felix had taken to leaving his fiddle in Nettie Mae's place at the table because he said it "looked just too *durned* lonely the way it was." He started cooking weird dishes with parsnips in them and saying things Nettie Mae used to say, like "Ain't that the purdiest thang you ever saw?" Some evenings I thought I could hear Nettie Mae whistling for Wilson and the back porch door creaking open. Felix heard things, too. He tried to explain it to me scientifically, but it was no use; we both knew it was some part of Nettie Mae staying behind to make sure we were all right. And I was glad of it.

I never went back to school. Shawnie came up once

a week. She brought her mama's homemade chicken soup and worried over us.

"You've both got to eat something," she scolded. "Now sit down and fill your bellies. I want this pot empty before I take it back home." Felix and I didn't have much appetite, but we ate for Shawnie's sake and sent her home with an empty pot and promises to get more sleep.

I didn't tell Shawnie about my bargain with the stars. I knew she'd be angry with me. I hadn't felt electric since that night. All was quiet. It was like having a house full of wild guests for months and months, and then finally everyone went home at the same time. It was a relief, but lonely, too, as if something important was missing. Everything seemed to be missing.

★   ★   ★

"Doesn't seem possible, does it, Harmony?" Felix said to me one night over dinner. "That she could be gone forever. That we'll never see her again." I got up from my chair and put my arm around Felix. He cried. I cried too. As we sat there holding on to each other, I knew what he meant about missing Nettie Mae. I kept thinking I'd see her any moment coming down the trail, or I'd turn the corner into the kitchen and she'd be where she always was—in front of a simmering pot, messing with some herbs. This must be what it's like to lose an arm or a leg, something that's been part of you forever. You keep looking for it even after it's gone.

The only thing that seemed to lift my spirits was the

thought of Caleb. Shawnie brought me a letter from him one afternoon along with a jar of homemade pickles and a pie.

"I didn't think that boy knew *how* to write," Shawnie said, handing me the small white envelope. "He's never written *me* a letter." I tucked the letter in my pocket.

Shawnie's face fell. "Aren't you going to open it?"

"Later. When I'm alone."

"Oh, come on, Harmony. He *is* my cousin, after all. I won't tell a soul." I raised my eyebrows. "I'll even spit on it."

"It's private, Shawnie."

"All right, don't open it, then. I bet I can guess what it says anyway. '*Oh, Harmony, I'm so in love with you . . . I can't sleep at night.*'" Shawnie burst into giggles.

"He is not in love with me," I protested. Shawnie hugged me to her and whispered in my ear. "You believe whatever you like, but I know love when I see it. And that boy is in love." I shrugged and looked at the ground, trying not to smile.

★   ★   ★

I opened my letter from Caleb that evening, after I'd sent Felix off to bed with a cup of warm milk. I sat down on the rug in front of the fireplace and wrapped Nettie Mae's shawl around my shoulders. It still smelled like her. Felix had kept all of Nettie Mae's things. He said he had no need to forget her and move on as some folks might suggest. "Nettie Mae was my true love, Harmony. That doesn't happen for many people. A person needs time to let that love settle into something else." With Nettie Mae's shawl wrapped around my shoulders, I felt like she was still with me.

Caleb's letter was brief. In fact, it was so short, I wasn't even sure it qualified as a letter at all. It was more like a postcard in an envelope.

Dear Harmony,

Shawnie told me about your aunt Nettie Mae. I wish I could be there. Planning to come up to your mountains for the reunion in one week. Hope I don't get a nosebleed. Will you meet me at Shawnie's? Please come.

I miss you,
Caleb

I thought about Caleb's mountain face as I read his short letter, and deep down in my belly, mingled with my sadness over Nettie Mae, was a feeling of excitement. I leaned my back against the legs of Felix's rocking chair and stared into the fire, and the flames shot high up into the chimney.

★

CHAPTER
FIFTEEN

★

AS SUMMER TOOK hold, Felix and I felt a new burst of energy come over us. Felix said maybe it was because of all of Shawnie's chicken soup, or because the days were so long and we had so much work to do to clean up the place. But I knew for me it was the anticipation of seeing Caleb that made me jump out of bed every morning instead of dragging myself around in a daze like I had been.

"You're all lit up, Harmony," Felix said to me the morning of the reunion as I poured hot water over my oats. I blushed a little.

"I'm off to the Pawletts' reunion. It's today, remember?"

"How could I forget?" Felix said with a twinkle in his eye. "Who's going to be there?"

"Oh, just Shawnie and a bunch of her cousins. You know, a whole crowd of folks. Shawnie said for you to come if you like."

Felix smiled. "Well, that's mighty nice of her, honey, but I have to keep working on the studio today. I'm almost done fixing the Harmony Box—a few more hours of tweaking and it'll be tuned to perfection. Besides, it'll be good for you to go on your own, be with your friends. It's been a long winter."

I smiled and gave Felix a kiss on the cheek. "I'll bring you home some cake. The Pawletts always have cake."

"That sounds just fine," Felix said.

It had been almost six months since I'd walked down the trail to the Hollow. It had never been that long before. It was a warm day and I'd decided to wear a sundress that had once belonged to Nettie Mae. It had a yellow background covered in rose flowers and vines. My legs had grown long over the winter, so the dress fell just above my knee. I looked good in yellow. It matched my hair. This was the very same dress Nettie Mae wore to the Huntsville Fair the day she met Felix. She'd left it for me, along with her tortoiseshell and a box full of pretty glass beads that had belonged to her grandmother McClean.

On any other beautiful summer day, I would have been smelling the new flowers on my way down the trail and taking my time, soaking in the sun—but not this day. I walked as quickly as I could because I didn't want to be late.

Halfway down the mountain, I was startled by a sound in the bushes—a low growl and then a whimper. I listened. The growl came again, and then silence. I walked off the path in the direction of the sound toward one of the narrow streams that ran down to the valley. It was the prettiest little stream, surrounded on all sides by shiny green myrtle. The sound came louder and as I moved closer, I could make out the tail and ears of a small coyote. A "coydog," Felix calls them. Its leg was caught in a steel trap. It looked up at me and I saw that its eyes were glazed over in pain. Steel leg traps are the cruelest things I know of—causing an animal to suffer until it dies. I'd come upon a red fox one spring that had died in a trap. The hunter had never even bothered to come back and check it.

I sat down on the other side of the stream and watched the coyote. I didn't want to get too near for fear of being bit, and I was pretty sure I wasn't strong enough to open the trap even if I could get close enough. Then the feeling came over me. My arms began to tingle all the way to my fingers and I thought I might cry or sing, or burst into flame. I'd thought it was gone forever. I'd thought the stars had heard my prayer and taken it from me that night.

The coyote began to bark suddenly. It was a loud, fierce sound. I had a strong urge to turn and run back to the safety of the trail, but then something made me think of Willa, and instead of running, I took the sound into me. I felt my fear and the coyote's fear. I wished myself peace and brought my attention to his yellow eyes. I tried to comfort him by keeping my gaze steady and peaceful, and he stopped barking. Then I focused on the trap. It didn't move, but I kept my thoughts steadily upon it. Finally it began to open, very slightly at first, then inch by inch, until the coyote could pull his leg free. He looked at me for only a moment, then turned and hobbled away.

I watched him until he disappeared behind a rock, then I let out a sigh of relief. The electric feeling subsided and I dipped my hand into the stream and splashed cold water on my face. I looked up at the sky, to the stars, which were always there even when I couldn't see them—and I thanked them for not listening to me on that dark night. Until this moment, I hadn't known what it would be like to live the rest of my life without that feeling. Now I knew I never wanted to. A part of me had been missing since the night I tried to give my gift back, and as I walked down the mountain, I felt whole again.

★   ★   ★

The Pawletts' house was around the corner from the school. It was a massive farmhouse with porches on all sides, and the yard was filled with huge white tents and children running everywhere.

I spotted Shawnie. She was leaning over the side of

the porch, talking to a boy with curly blond hair. She looked up as I came closer.

"Harmony!" she yelled, running toward me. She grabbed me around the waist and kissed me on the cheek. "I knew you'd come."

"I wouldn't miss this," I said, looking around.

"No, he's not here." Shawnie poked me in the arm. "His mama takes forever to get going, and my uncle Carlton has a terrible sense of direction. They're always late. Drives Caleb crazy. But I'm glad they're not here yet. I want to have you to myself for a little while. It's hard being friends with someone who's in love. You're always half here and half looking for my cousin."

"I'm sorry," I said.

"That's okay. I don't take it personally. It's not your fault anyway. You see, these endorphins get released in your brain when you're in love. It's like eating twelve chocolate bars all at the same time. Add a few out-of-control hormones to the picture and it can turn a perfectly rational person into a distracted, raving lunatic."

I rolled my eyes. "Shawnie, sometimes I think you make this stuff up."

"I'd never make up something like that," she said seriously. "It's the truth. Sometimes the truth is stranger than real life. Come on," she said, pulling me toward the picnic tables. "I'm starving. Even people in love have to eat."

We spent the whole afternoon together, eating and catching up on the news of the Hollow, but she was right. It was hard to give her my full attention. I always had one eye peeled for Caleb.

We tried to wait to have dinner with him, but the food was going fast, so at six o'clock we sat down under a beech tree and joined in. I wasn't very hungry. Thinking about Caleb must've taken my appetite away. But I did have a little bit of roast chicken and potatoes and a small piece of chocolate cake. I guess every family specializes in something, and the Pawletts specialize in cakes. There must have been eight different kinds.

Even though the light lasts longer in June, the days eventually get dark, and it was an hour's walk back up the trail. I didn't want Felix worrying about me and I don't like walking the trails alone at night. If I'd had Wilson with me, I would have stayed later, but by eight o'clock I decided to go. It began to look like Caleb might not come at all.

"I don't know what happened to them," Shawnie said. She seemed upset.

"I just hope he's okay."

"Oh, he's okay. Until he gets here, he's okay. Then I'm going to wring his neck."

I laughed, but I was disappointed. "Well," I said. "Maybe I'll see him again sometime."

"You will. I can guarantee that."

I gave her a hug and she handed me a huge piece of strawberry cake for Felix. I started back home, my heart heavy as a stone. *What could have kept him?* I wondered.

★　★　★

About halfway up the trail, I heard Wilson barking, or at least it sounded like Wilson. It was hard to tell. The barking echoed around me. That happens the closer you get to the Hollow—things echo more. I stood still and looked up through the trees at the sky. I had enough time to get home before it got completely dark, but the light was beginning to fade and I had to watch my footing. It's easy when you're tired to trip on a root if you're not paying attention. And I was tired. Tired of waiting for things to change, for something good to happen.

The barking became louder. It sounded like it was coming from two directions. Ahead of me, it sounded like Wilson, and below me, another dog. There *are* some wild dogs up in the mountains. Hunting dogs that ran away or got lost and learned to survive. Usually they don't bother people. They only go after rabbits and other dogs. But still, they can be fierce. *Just what I need to end this disappointing day*, I thought, *to get eaten by a wild dog.*

Gradually I could see a lantern coming up the trail behind me, swinging back and forth. And another lantern was coming down the trail.

"Harmony?" a voice called. It sounded like Caleb. And then I heard another voice calling my name that sounded like Felix. I decided to stay right where I was and wait to see what was going on. I hadn't brought a lantern, because I thought I'd be home long before dark. Caleb and Shawnie's hound, Bracken, reached me first.

"Caleb! What are you doing here?" He didn't answer. He stopped to catch his breath; then he reached out his hand and pulled me toward him and kissed me, knocking the cake out of my hand and onto the ground. It was not at all like the gentle kiss on the Ferris wheel that I wasn't sure had happened. This was a serious kiss. Hard and long. It felt like someone had taken a match and lit my insides on fire. Caleb only let go when Wilson appeared, knocking into his legs as he and Bracken sniffed each other and wolfed down Felix's piece of strawberry cake.

"Harmony?" It was Felix. I pulled away from Caleb and turned around to see Felix smiling shyly in the shadows. "Mighty sorry to disturb you," he said, looking down at the ground. "I thought Harmony was alone. Just came down to walk her home. But . . . I see she's in good hands."

I let go of Caleb's hand and walked toward Felix. "This is my friend, Caleb Pawlett," I explained. "Shawnie's cousin. We spent the day together at the Huntsville Fair."

Felix stepped up and extended his hand to Caleb, smiling widely. "Well, son, I'd say that's a mighty fine place to spend a day with someone."

★ ★ ★

Caleb walked me the rest of the way home while Felix went on ahead with Wilson and Bracken. I had so much to tell Caleb that I talked the whole way. I told him about saving the trees and losing Nettie Mae, and everything in between—the feelings, the dreams. Every once in a while we'd stop, and I'd look over at him and he'd grab my hand and hold it. He understood, without saying a word.

He walked me all the way to my front door, kissed me on the front porch and then stuck his head inside and said good night to Felix before heading back down the mountain with Bracken leading the way. I wasn't sure when I'd see Caleb again, but it made me happy knowing he was out there in the world, thinking of me. And I felt electric thinking of him. As electric as I had when I'd helped the coyote, another gift I would never wish away.

★

CHAPTER
SIXTEEN

★

FELIX FINISHED GATHERING up the pieces of the
Harmony Box and put it back together as good as new. I
was feeling more and more restless as summer wore on,
and so was Felix. One afternoon, we were sitting on the
front porch looking out at the Old People and Felix said,
"Harmony, I think it's about time we got off this mountain. We need a change of scenery."

"Really? Are you sure, Felix?" We'd been so busy
and so many things had changed, I thought maybe he
had forgotten about our dream of traveling.

"What about Austria?"

I stared at him. I'd told him about the woman in Austria whom Shawnie had been corresponding with all winter long. "How would we get to Austria?" I asked him.

He smiled and held out one of Nettie Mae's leather pouches, labeled TRAVELING FUNDS. "Nettie left us enough here to get to Timbuktu and back. I think it will get us to Austria." He winked and I agreed, as long as we could stop and see Caleb on the way.

★ ★ ★

A week before we were to leave the mountain, a sweet-smelling letter arrived from Burston Jones, informing us that the Great Northern Lumber Company of Tallahassee, Florida, had declared lot number 3098 inhospitable for harvesting and had purchased a piece of land in Texas instead.

"Inhospitable!" Felix said, shaking his head. "I'd say we were mighty hospitable to those loggers, wouldn't you? Went through a dozen eggs a day, didn't we?"

"I think he meant the *land* was inhospitable, Felix, not us."

Felix winked. "Well, I always said, this land was only meant for old stubborn Cherokee women and brilliant scientists."

★ ★ ★

Our last night on the mountain was clear, and the sky was full of stars. Felix and I climbed the rise loaded down with his telescope and the Harmony Box. Felix believed that if the weather held, this August would be the clearest Perseid showers ever, and the rise was the best place in the world to view them. We wanted to remember the night I arrived in the midst of shooting stars.

We took our places on a flat rock, spread a blanket beneath us and ate some cake. I put on Felix's headset, and he peered through the long cylinder of his telescope.

I'd only worn Felix's headset at home, but up here, it was spectacular. All the beauty of the night, without any sound. Only an occasional blip of static would come over the airways, breaking the silence. I was a little afraid at first to wear the headset because of my history with electronic devices, but Felix assured me that I would be fine.

I felt a soft touch on my sleeve. Felix was pointing up toward the Milky Way. A shooting star streaked across the sky. I caught the tail of it as it disappeared into the darkness. Maybe it turned back into dust, or maybe it crashed to earth. You never know what paths stars will take.

I fiddled with the dials of the Harmony Box, having no idea of what I was doing and getting mostly static. It was like a radio I was trying to tune to a good station. I expected Merle Haggard or Kenny Rogers to come on at any moment. And then suddenly, a sound broke the static. Distant, but clear. It was singing. But not Merle Haggard, and not planets. Not a hum or vibration like Felix says it's supposed to sound like either, but a woman's voice. A voice singing in Cherokee. It couldn't be mistaken.

I grabbed Felix's hand and pointed to my ears. "I

can hear it, Felix! I can hear it!" I yelled. His eyes widened and he waited for me to explain. But then it was gone before I could take the headset off. The static returned, thicker this time, like a television coming on after a power outage. Felix took the headset and put it on, fiddled with the dials. He said he heard nothing. Nothing but the wind.

★   ★   ★

When I was little, Nettie Mae used to tell me the story of the star child, Polaris. She said that every person is like the North Star when they first come into the world—bright and full of light. If you hide that light under a basket it grows dim, but if you have the courage to live the life you were born to live, it stays bright. That's what I was thinking the night Felix sat listening to the wind through his headset.

Maybe it was a gift I was given a long time ago from a family I never met, somewhere out in the heavens, that enabled me to hear what Felix couldn't, or maybe it was my love for the family that had raised me. But I know what I heard. I know what came over the airways that night as sure as I've known anything. It was Nettie Mae singing her turtle song, followed by the rush of the wind. And for a moment, we were together again. The three of us. Passing by one another—close enough to make music.

ABOUT THE AUTHOR

RITA MURPHY lives in Vermont with her husband and their son. *Night Flying*, her first novel, won the 1999 Delacorte Press Prize for a First Young Adult Novel and made her a *Publishers Weekly* Flying Start Author. She has also written *Black Angels*, a coming-of-age novel set against the backdrop of the fledgling civil rights movement. She is at work on her next novel.